LUST ON THE REBOUND

MANDY MICHELLE

Amazon ISBN: 9798398572742

Ingrams ISBN: 9781953100573

Cover Design: Dreams2Media

Editor: Ezra O'Neil

First Trade Paperback Printing by Scarsdale Publishing. Ltd. August 2023

10 9 8 7 6 5 4 3 2

ACKNOWLEDGMENTS

The Missoulian
Heineken
Led Zeppelin
Jeep
VW Beetle
The Creature from the Black Lagoon
Lexus LS
West Glacier Mercantile
Teflon
Spice Girls
Marilyn Monroe
BMW
Chevy
Maserati
Missoula Police Department
Freddie Kreuger
The Hulk
Northern Rockies Medical Center
Ten Spoon Vineyard

*Dad, one day I will write a book I'll let you read.
(But if you do read this one, please skip Chapters 2, 15, 21 and 22.)*

CHAPTER ONE

IT WAS WELL PAST MIDNIGHT WHEN KYLA FINALLY MADE IT HOME FROM the wedding. At only twenty-four, she should have been embarrassed by how much her back ached lugging her camera gear up three flights of stairs, but she hadn't been named Montana's best wedding photographer by *The Missoulian* two years running for nothing. Despite her exhaustion, she knew she'd captured some beautiful moments tonight. Her couple would be thrilled.

She reached her apartment door, set her camera bag on the floor, and fished for her keys in her purse. As she searched, her phone vibrated under her fingers. She flipped it over with a tired sigh as Alan's third call of the day rang through.

She was almost proud of his restraint today. She'd gotten six calls and thirteen texts yesterday, eleven calls and seventeen texts the day before. Maybe he got the hint she didn't want him back.

Of course, she'd found that folded piece of stationary from his company wedged under her windshield wiper when she left that afternoon. She could see indents of writing through the paper, but she hadn't opened it. Instead, Kyla had pocketed it to show Dylan, her neighbor, best friend, and personal boy in blue. Alan hadn't crossed any legal lines yet, but if he did, Dylan would protect her. He always had.

She finally found her keys and fumbled them into the lock, then froze when the door creaked open under the gentle pressure. A small chunk of wood fell out of the doorframe. Her heart jumped into overdrive.

She peered around the open door, down the short hallway, and into the empty living room. Nothing seemed obviously out of place.

Kyla took one shaky step into the apartment, then stepped back out. Now that she looked closer, a piece of her doorframe lay on the ground, and the knob twisted at a slightly awkward angle. She hadn't just forgotten to lock her door.

She pulled her phone back out and dialed Dylan's number.

A hand closed over her shoulder. Kyla yelped.

"Rosy?"

She spun around to find Dylan looking at her with worry in his eyes, and she pressed a hand to her pounding heart. "Jesus, Dill."

He winked at her, like always, and leaned in to press a kiss to the top of her head. At a solid foot taller than she was, with shoulders wide as a linebacker's, he should have cut an intimidating figure in the dimly lit hallway, but she had adored him from the moment he volunteered to help her move into her apartment three years ago.

"What's wrong?" he asked. "Rough night?"

She shook her head, reached for his hand, and nodded at the door. "Someone was inside."

He twisted his face into a rare frown and released her hand to check out the door. "Fuck. You think it was Alan?"

She nodded when he looked at her over his shoulder. "He left this on my windshield." Kyla proffered the folded paper.

Dylan reached into the pocket of his suit jacket and slipped on a pair of nitrile gloves before delicately taking the paper and unfolding it. She noticed he still wore his work clothes, a nice charcoal suit. He must have gotten in late, too. Detectives never worked regular hours.

He furrowed his brow as he scanned the paper. "Have you read this?"

Kyla shook her head. "I don't really want to hear what he has to say."

That had been true earlier, but now she was genuinely scared. In the hallway light, she could see large, dark letters on the other side of the paper.

Dylan looked up at her. "Are you sure?"

Kyla nodded resolutely. Dylan refolded the paper and handed it back to her.

"Hold onto that." He glanced inside her open door again. "And wait in the hallway." He gave her a reassuring smile but pushed aside his suit jacket to access the gun on his hip. "I'll check it out to make sure your apartment's empty."

Kyla paced the hall while she waited for the all-clear. She tried to keep her breathing steady. Usually, she didn't spook like this, but since she'd caught her fiancé with his secretary a month and a half ago, nothing had been okay. He hadn't accepted her engagement ring back. He hadn't stopped calling or texting. He'd left that note that made Dylan appear so worried. *No* seemed to have left Alan's vocabulary.

But she never thought he would go as far as breaking into her apartment.

Her stomach roiled. How long had Dylan been gone? Minutes? Hours?

A low, muffled voice reached her through the walls of her apartment, and her heart thudded. That had to be Dylan, right? Who could he be talking to?

Finally, when she felt about to burst with nervous energy, Dylan re-emerged. "Kyla…" He lifted a hand as if to touch her arm, but he ran it through his light hair. "No one's inside. But someone definitely was."

"Why?" Her breath caught in her throat, and the hall spun. "Was something messed up? Or missing? What's going on?"

"Just wait." He pulled his phone from his back pocket and sent a text. "I have a team on the way. They're going to check everything out."

Kyla's brain whirred out of control, and she began pacing again. Someone had broken into her home. Her home! She hadn't seen the bathroom, the kitchen, or the bedroom. Had they taken her jewelry? Had two different criminals broken in at once, fought, and now there was a body on her bed? What could possibly make Dylan look at her with that level of concern in his warm, blue eyes?

"Can you please tell me what's going on here? I'm imagining worst-case scenarios."

Dylan took a deep breath. "There's some damage, but I *think* the only thing taken was the contents of your…underwear drawer."

She skidded to a halt, all her panicked ideas crashing down around her. "My *what*?"

"I can show you after the crime scene crew arrives, but we have to wait until then. We don't want to lose any evidence. And you should give them that letter." Dylan scooped up the camera gear still sitting in the hallway. "Let's wait at my place."

"Do you need to handle this?" she asked. "I know you just got off shift, but this seems like it's in your jurisdiction."

He shook his head. "Nope. They couldn't drag me back on the clock if they begged."

She nodded and waited while he unlocked his apartment

door. Thor, his nine-month-old Belgian Malinois puppy, rushed out, wiggling and waggling all over her.

"Hi, muffin." Kyla sat on the floor just inside the apartment door, let the dog climb on her lap, then snuggled her face in his soft fur. Finally, her heartbeat began to slow. She always relaxed with Thor around.

"I'm going to go wait in the hall, okay?" Dylan asked. "You're okay with Thor?"

"Of course." Kyla massaged the puppy's ears as he twisted around to lick her face. "You're such a good boy, Thor. Yes, you are. You don't listen to them. You're not a police dropout. You're a star pet. That's right. Yes, you are."

Thor hadn't stopped licking her face by the time Dylan returned. Kyla looked up at him. Dylan's face remained creased with a frown. "How bad is it?"

"Come on." He grasped her hand and pulled her to her feet. "I'll show you."

Kyla closed the door on Thor and followed Dylan back into her apartment. Just like she'd originally thought, not a thing looked out of place in the entrance or living room. A crime scene tech stopped Kyla just long enough to take Alan's note from her, then Kyla and Dylan walked into her room together.

Her stomach flipped. A hurricane had hit her bedroom. Clothes covered her plum-colored, satin sheets. Her underwear drawer stood open and clearly empty. All the mirrors and her lamp were smashed. Black fingerprint dust coated her dresser and the windowsill that led to the fire escape. Huge letters, written in red, covered the wall above her bed.

MINE.

Dylan nodded at the message. "That covers the gist of that note Alan left you."

If any doubt had remained, it all disappeared as she realized what lay on top of the other clothes on her bed. An overwhelming desire to cry rushed to the surface as she crossed the room on shaky legs to run a hand over the satin and lace of the wedding dress she never got to wear.

She remembered her best friend's champagne-scented laughter in the wedding boutique as Kyla spent hours trying on options. Alan had been a traditionalist, so the final product was more conservative than Kyla would've chosen otherwise, but she'd fallen in love with the lacy sleeves and enormous train.

Something cool touched her finger, and she closed her hand around her engagement ring.

"What is it?" Dylan asked.

She opened her fingers, and they looked at the half-carat ring on her sweaty palm.

"So, this isn't about theft." Dylan had donned gloves at some point, and he plucked the ring out of her hand carefully before bagging it. "Why do you still have it?"

Kyla shook her head. "He wouldn't take it back." She sat down beside her dress, and the tears bubbled over.

She'd planned the perfect event. Church first, Alan's idea, then to an outside area for the reception. In June, the weather should have been wonderful. Kyla had spent months dreaming about the way her face would hurt from smiling, and she already had a space reserved in her freezer to keep a piece of the wedding cake.

Alan had taken that from her, with his wandering eyes and hands and—

Dylan reached for her hand and pulled her to her feet. "Come on. No tears."

She wrapped her arms around his waist and buried her face against his chest. "Will you sell all this stuff?"

"The dress?"

She nodded. "And the ring. I want all reminders of Alan out of my home."

He rubbed her back. "Done. Just come back to my place. I'll sort it all out, Rosy."

"I hate that nickname, Dill." Another tear slid down her cheek.

"What? Rosy?" He brushed the tear away. "You love it."

She shrugged.

"I hate that this happened to you." Dylan squeezed her. "You don't take shit from anyone, especially me. I'll deal with this nobody with a panty fetish."

A shiver ran through Kyla's body, and she pulled back. "You're purposefully not saying his name. Do you think Alan will escalate beyond this?" She looked at the writing on the wall. Lipstick? Paint? "Do you think I'm in danger?"

"I won't let him touch you." Dylan's gaze became iron. "Now, put on your PJs and come home with me. Thor will give you some more lovin' while we catch up on *Model Madness.*"

She leaned into him, overcome by the desire to cry again. Kyla opened her mouth to accept the invitation but shook her head. She didn't crumble like this when things got tough. Even though she felt a little fragile right then, she faced her problems head-on.

She pulled back. "Thanks, but I need to clean up first."

"After, then?" He locked his gaze with hers.

"Are you just asking me over so I'll bring peanut butter cups?"

Dylan pressed a kiss to her forehead, lingering a second longer than expected. "That goes without saying."

* * *

An hour later, Kyla zipped the wedding dress into the garment bag, stuffed it into the back of the closet and turned around to survey her work. Bed, clear. Floor, clear. Dresser—well, not clear. She'd never be organized enough for that, but she'd gotten everything back into its proper place, at least. She turned in a slow circle, rubbing her arms to chase away goose bumps. Kyla had been awake for nearly twenty-four hours. She was so exhausted, but she knew she wouldn't sleep. Not when Alan was out there.

She changed into sweats and a T-shirt, then headed for Dylan's. He'd kept the door unlocked for her, so she breezed in without knocking, though she made a point to lock the door behind her. Kyla dropped a plastic baggie of her homemade peanut butter cups on the coffee table in front of Dylan's couch next to a box of cookies and two bottles of Heineken. Then, she threw herself down on the couch beside him. Thor jumped up onto her lap and rested his head on her chest. She took a deep breath. She could relax. She could be normal.

"For me?" She nodded toward the nearest bottle of Heineken on the table.

"Yep," he said.

She grabbed the bottle and took a big swig. Dylan dug a few peanut butter cups from the bag and popped one into his mouth before passing them to her. A girl could do worse than end a day drowning her sorrows in cheap beer and chocolate. She grabbed a peanut butter cup and took a bite. Thor's eyes locked onto it, and he wagged his tail.

"No chocolate for you." She kissed his nose, then nodded at the cookies and quirked an eyebrow at Dylan. "From your brother's kickass bakery?"

Dylan grunted. "He drops a box off at the station every Friday."

Kyla reached for one, took a bite, and groaned. "Oh, my gosh, Dylan. I think these are better than sex."

"I've never had any complaints." He smirked.

Kyla rolled her eyes, then let Thor lick the cookie crumbs

from her fingers. "Are you ever going to tell me why your brother keeps giving you cookies you don't eat?"

"No." Dylan grabbed another peanut butter cup. "See that girl?" He nodded at his fifty-inch screen and the show playing on it. "She's getting the boot this week—no connection to the camera at all. Of course, you're the photographer, but am I right?"

Kyla let the show unfold for a few minutes, then nodded though her mind wasn't on the program. Instead, she couldn't stop thinking of her ex-fiancé. Even after everything, she couldn't believe Alan had ransacked her apartment and left her dress on the bed. It was a message. He wanted her back and was tired of her ignoring his calls and text messages.

When they'd met in line at the grocery store, he'd stumbled over his words. He had been sweet and shy. Adorable. The break-in felt completely out of character, but how could she argue with the evidence, and if she were to believe the evidence, then how could she have been engaged to a man who would do this to her?

"I don't know how I'm going to sleep over there."

"Me either," Dylan said. "Do you need a bodyguard tonight? I can sleep on the sofa if you want."

Kyla sighed and settled deeper into the couch. If she couldn't be happy right now, at least Dylan made her feel safe. He always did. He checked for mice and comforted her when deals fell through, whereas Alan had been so busy over the last year it was as if tax season stretched across the whole twelve months.

"Maybe for one night. Or a week." She cracked a rusty smile.

Dylan put a hand over his heart. "It's my job to serve and protect."

Kyla's shoulders finally relaxed in the peace of Dylan's

apartment. She pointed to the TV. "That photographer is hand-some, in a rugged sort of way."

Dylan shrugged. "I guess."

"Oh, c'mon. Square jaw, crooked nose, dark eyes with a story behind them."

Dylan didn't take his eyes off the show. "You're looking again?"

She laughed. "I don't know if I'm *looking*. Like, I miss the…"

"Sex?"

She shook her head and rubbed Thor's ears. "Maybe. But I don't miss the drama, you know?"

Dylan popped another peanut butter cup into his mouth and shook his head. "Well, if you want a rebound guy, I'll set you up with someone."

"Ha. I'd love to see what you think is a good setup for me."

An obnoxious porn star ringtone sounded from Dylan's pocket. He pulled the phone out, checked the display, then hit ignore.

"Adriana?" Kyla asked as she wove her fingers into Thor's fur.

"Nope."

"Amber? Brittney?"

Dylan grimaced. "You're making me sound bad."

"I am not." She paused. "Holly?"

"Ding, ding, ding, ding."

Kyla smiled. "I thought we liked Holly. She was, um, bubbly."

Thor licked her cheek and thumped his tail against the back of the couch.

"*We* didn't like Holly," he said. "*You* liked Holly."

Kyla grinned. Usually, he tried to stop her from meeting his flavor-of-the-month girls, but Kyla had run into Holly when arriving home late from a wedding shoot. "She had pretty shoes." And big, big breasts. "I don't have a love life. I'm living vicariously through yours."

Dylan rolled his eyes.

"At least Holly's loyal." She began ticking things off on her fingers. "And committed. I wish..."

"Alan was an asshole. Forget him."

Thor jumped down to get a drink of water, and Kyla immediately missed his heat on her body. She shivered. "Don't be mad, but I think I miss him. Well, not the way he's acting now, but I miss the way we used to be."

"You don't. You miss the security you *thought* he gave you." Dylan took her hand and pulled her next to him. She blinked sleepily and pillowed her head on his chest. She couldn't exactly disagree, but she didn't feel like being lectured. Again.

"—and he knew about the thing with your dad. He knew, and he did it anyway. You gotta stop letting him take up space in your life."

A month and a half ago, she'd caught Alan sleeping with his secretary, invited him to a fancy dinner, then dumped him in public so maybe she wouldn't cry quite as severely. Of course, she'd broken down weeping. Dylan had been the one she'd called to drive her home when she realized she couldn't see through the tears, and he'd even gotten them takeout before they left. Having a man for a best friend had never felt strange. They confided in each other, shared their dreams, and vented about rough days at work. Sometimes, though, he didn't realize when she didn't want advice.

She glanced back at Dylan. "Alan never liked you." She was being petty, but she needed him to stop harping about Alan.

"I can't help it if my adorable dimples scared him away."

Maybe she'd been wrong to have kept her friendship with Dylan while knowing his presence in her life bothered Alan. They fought about him, but should a girl have to give up her best friend for a fiancé who never really showed up? Kyla should have seen the warning signs long before the affair. He'd even refused to move in with her when she asked.

"Maybe I should have—"

"Should have what?" Dylan asked. "Stayed with a guy who got jealous over your friendships while he was fucking his secretary?"

Kyla sat up. "You're being a dick. I was going to say I should have ended things with him long ago."

"All right, all right." Dylan put his hands up. "I just don't like seeing you this upset over someone who isn't worth it."

Thor trotted back into the room and plopped down on the carpet beside Dylan. He scratched Thor between the ears. "Did you call your mom? Let her know what happened?"

"No. She wouldn't have picked up, anyway. She's tired of listening to me complain about Alan."

"She would have. She loves you, even if you disagree sometimes."

Kyla sighed. "She makes me feel crazy. My engagement is over, and I have to move on, but she won't let me."

"You're not crazy." He wrapped his arms around her.

She loved his hugs, even though she now smelled more like Dylan's strong, spicy cologne than he did.

"You are smart and beautiful and funny and talented. And, let's be honest, Kyla, you have an incredible ass."

That made her laugh—obviously his plan all along. Kyla looked up into his stunning blue eyes. Her pulse skipped a beat. Did she see desire? He dropped his gaze to her mouth. She licked her lips as heat seared through her veins. She hadn't been looked at with such hunger in a long time.

Alan had never looked at her that way. Until now, neither had Dylan.

"Why can't you be Mr. Right?" The words tumbled out of her mouth, wanton and breathy.

She'd never acted this way with Dylan before. Sure, he was gorgeous, but she'd always considered him perfect friend material. Since the breakup, her world had narrowed to her pain. She filled all her time with photography, jogging, and walking Thor. Anything and everything but her sexual desires. Now, she found herself in the arms of a man, beautiful on the inside and out. It would be so easy to love him...

He leaned in, and Kyla stared in surprise. He closed his eyes and brushed his lips across hers before he lazily dragged his tongue over her bottom lip.

Kyla pulled back. "Dylan Hamilton, you just licked me."

He opened his eyes. "That is a legitimate move. Ask Holly." He gathered her closer. "Come here."

Dylan covered her mouth with his and slid his tongue inside. He tasted like peanut butter, chocolate, and beer. Delicious—but weird.

He tangled his tongue with hers, clearly knowing how to kiss, but he was her best friend. After a moment, Kyla broke the kiss.

Dylan opened his eyes and rubbed the back of his neck. "No?"

"I love you, Dill." She licked her lips. "But I don't think so."

He smiled, and her best friend, the trustworthy, comfortable guy she loved, reappeared. She wanted this Dylan, not the dominant, kissing version.

He shrugged and ran a hand through his hair. "Me, neither. Nothing moved downstairs, if you know what I mean."

She nodded, and he winked. "Sorry about that. I've always been curious."

"It's okay. You don't need to apologize." Tensions had run high all evening, and she understood. After a moment, she snuggled into the couch next to him, and he wrapped an arm comfortably around her shoulders. They watched another episode of *Model Madness* in easy silence.

"Do you remember what I suggested after you dumped Alan?" Dylan asked as the episode drew to a close.

"To run away and hide in your brother's cabin in the oh-so-beautiful mountains of Glacier National Park?"

"I'm impressed. You do listen." He rubbed her arm. "Josh has a nice place, and I don't know when we're gonna be able to get the lock fixed, so just take my spare key and head up first thing tomorrow morning. Take Thor for company,"

"Are you trying to get rid of me?" She sat up and looked him straight in the eye. "Wait. Are things weird between us now?"

Dylan kissed her forehead. "No to both questions. I love you, Kyla, but as we just saw, platonically. I want you safe, and I want to be able to focus on who broke into your apartment."

"You're the best cop in town. I'm not scared." A lie.

Kyla didn't have a wedding to shoot for another week, so she could disappear to the woods just long enough for Dylan to arrest Alan so she could go back to sleeping soundly in her bed.

A little escape from the city would be nice.

CHAPTER TWO

JOSH STRAIGHTENED HIS TIE AS HE ENTERED THE DOWNTOWN ITALIAN restaurant where he was supposed to meet Natasha for dinner an hour ago. "Reservation for Josh Hamilton," he said to the pretty, red-headed hostess who greeted him.

This afternoon, he'd had a brilliant idea about ice cream flavors as cookies, and he'd just nailed down a recipe for rocky road when he pulled his head out of the industrial mixer and realized six hours had passed. Natasha hadn't answered any of the apology texts he'd sent during the last fifteen minutes, so he had no idea if she'd still be here. She always got so mad when he was late, but he never forgot to text, so he really didn't get the fuss.

The hostess offered a sympathetic smile. "Your party left half an hour ago, sir."

Josh winced. "I figured as much. Thanks."

He headed back outside to his Jeep, then pulled into traffic.

Damn Tasha. He knew he'd fucked up, but he couldn't help being a little irritated. Establishing a new business took work—and time. The first three years had been fairly smooth, but in the last year, business had really started booming, and he wanted to keep up that momentum. She knew that. Or he thought she did.

He had only been with Tasha for about six months, but he wouldn't have stayed with her if he didn't care about her and didn't think they could build something. They were even heading up to his cabin in Glacier National Park for some time alone tomorrow—their first trip as a couple.

The cabin had always felt like a home away from home, and he wanted to share it with her. She couldn't accuse him of being all work, all the time after that.

Granted, he hadn't been up to the cabin in the last year except for basic maintenance, and he missed it, so maybe his motive for going up there held a tiny amount of selfishness.

He called Natasha on hands-free, but the call went right to voicemail.

Josh parked and rested his head against the steering wheel of the Jeep. He didn't feel like getting screamed at, but he really didn't want to cancel this trip. He hadn't seen a tree in far too long.

Josh stepped out, closed the door, and rehearsed his apology. Natasha tended to be high maintenance, bordering on needy, so he had some groveling to do.

He and Tasha had been hot and heavy since she, his favorite bank teller, had invited him to coffee out of the blue. The sex alone would've made her attitude worth it, but she was funny, smart, and looked incredible in those business suits.

Josh entered the building, strode past an army of fake potted ferns, and stopped at the fourth door on the left. She'd given him a key a few weeks ago, and he unlocked her door with an apology on his lips.

"Oh, Eric. Just like that," Tasha moaned.

What the hell?

Josh's legs moved on instinct, carrying him through the living room, down the hallway, and to the room he'd woken up in that morning. The door stood slightly ajar, giving him a perfect view of his girlfriend's toned legs wrapped around another man's naked waist.

Josh's vision tinged red, and he grabbed the doorframe to steady himself. "Looks like I missed dessert."

Natasha shrieked. The man fucking her twisted to look over his shoulder at Josh.

A memory exploded across Josh's mind. Himself in the man's position. Dylan in his. He shook his head.

Natasha shoved the stranger off, stood, and wrapped the silken bedsheet around herself. "Baby—"

Josh shot her a cold look. "Save it, Tash."

"Joshy." She pouted. "This isn't what it looks like."

"It's exactly what it looks like," the other man said. He folded his arms behind his head and made no effort to hide his naked body.

Tasha reached for Josh, and the sheet slipped to expose a tantalizing sliver of skin.

"Don't fucking touch me right now," Josh snapped. She withdrew her hands but didn't back off.

He stalked to the front door, and Tasha trailed behind like a lost puppy. "He doesn't mean anything, Joshy, I swear. He's no one."

His heart pounded. How long had she been cheating? How had he missed this?

"Baby, please," she begged. "This was one time. It was a mistake. I only met him 'cause you were late—"

"Don't." They reached the front door. "It was an hour. Don't fucking put this on me."

Josh threw open the apartment door, then stormed out of the building. He reached into his front jacket pocket for his phone to call someone and realized he didn't have anyone to call. Or at least not anyone who would pick up.

He flung himself into his car. He could slam a six-pack just as well by himself.

* * *

BY THE TIME SUMMER SUNLIGHT STREAMED THROUGH HIS OPEN bedroom window, Josh had gotten sick of his self-pity even though anger still simmered close to the surface. He ran a hand through his hair, then grabbed his phone off the nightstand and dialed his brother's number.

Dylan's phone rang three times before it went to voicemail. Josh didn't really know what he expected. Dylan never picked up when Josh called, preferring to text after discovering what Josh wanted.

"Hey, it's Josh. I broke things off with Tasha last night. I'm pretty sure I texted you about her. Maybe not. Anyway. I need space, so I'm headed up to the cabin for the weekend. Mountain air and all that good stuff." Josh slid out of bed and stopped short at the sight of Tasha's red bra dangling from his doorknob. "I made you a dozen pistachio macarons, as promised. Pick them up at the bakery anytime. Romeo is watching the counter, and he knows you're coming. Uh, I guess that's it. Oh, and I'm shutting off my phone. I don't want to be hounded by Tasha all weekend. Maybe we can grab a beer next week?"

Josh ended the call and shook his head. How many times had he asked Dylan to hang out over the past seven years? The most he'd gotten was occasional run-ins at the grocery store or when he dropped off cookies at the police station.

Still, he wouldn't stop asking. He wouldn't give up on the only family he had left.

He threw Tasha's bra in the garbage and pulled out a duffel bag. This weekend would be good for him—a much-needed break from work, women, and drama.

"Dammit." Josh slammed his hand down on the steering wheel. "Stop thinking about her."

He dialed up the Jeep's stereo to drown the memory of Natasha's cry of pleasure as another man fucked her.

He'd done his best to be good to her. Sure, he'd been late a few times or forgotten things she asked him to do, but he always made up for it by taking her on nice dates and buying her pretty things, so he hadn't seen this coming. Granted, girls had left him before, so Tasha dumping him probably shouldn't have been such a surprise. The cheating was new, though.

Damn it. Why couldn't he seem to find a woman who appreciated the time and effort it took to build a business from the bottom up?

Josh huffed out a breath and tried to let the blaring guitar and thudding drumbeats of Led Zeppelin distract him.

Maybe he should check his messages. Maybe Tasha had called to beg forgiveness with a seriously good explanation.

God, he really had become a sucker. He should've thrown his phone off a cliff.

He'd thought the mountain views of the park would relax him, but the tension in his shoulders didn't release until he turned onto his backroad. Josh loved his bakery, but nothing felt quite as much like home as this cabin. The Hamiltons had come up every summer when he and Dylan were kids, and he had nothing but fond memories. This had been his mom's place first, and she'd love that he had made the cabin his.

He slowed as he pulled up to his driveway and found a bubble-gum pink VW Beetle parked in his spot.

"Shit."

The only other person with keys to the cabin was Dylan, but as far as Josh knew, the guy hadn't set foot in the place in at least a decade, and that definitely wasn't Dylan's car or a car Josh could imagine anyone other than a girl driving. He couldn't believe his brother would just hand out the keys to the cabin without at least mentioning it. Then again, Dylan hardly spoke to him, so Josh shouldn't be so surprised. Hell, maybe Dylan had brought a girl up here. With the bakery taking over Josh's life, Dylan likely assumed Josh would never know.

His heart panged. He really needed to fix things with his big brother. His absence from Josh's life had started to wear on him. He missed Dylan more than he thought possible.

Josh parked and contemplated whether to head inside or leave. He'd wanted time alone, but maybe this was his chance to talk to Dylan, clear the air between them.

He got out of his Jeep, shouldered his duffle, and tried the door to the cabin. Locked. Josh unlocked it and stomped inside.

Empty grocery bags littered the counter, and a dog bed and bowls crowded the kitchen floor. Dylan had a puppy now. Odin? Zeus? No, Thor. Women's flip-flops sat by the door, but the cabin seemed quiet. A quick walkthrough of the lower floor came up empty.

Weird.

He dropped his bag on the sofa, then took the stairs two at a time to his bedroom. The door stood open, and clothes covered his bed. He spotted a least three pairs of shoes on the floor and what might have been the corner of a fourth. A teddy bear peeked out of the top of an overturned bag. A silky, pale pink robe, pretty and feminine, dangled off the inside doorknob.

He didn't see any of Dylan's clothes. Or any men's clothes.

Josh scrubbed a hand over his face. He needed to figure out who Goldilocks was and why she had taken over his bed, his cabin, and his weekend.

CHAPTER THREE

Kyla and Thor panted as they made their way up the path to the back of the cabin. After putting away the groceries she'd brought, the summer sun had beckoned her outside, but on their walk along a marked trailhead that ran beside the water, the air had warmed enough that she and the pup were sweating.

A hawk screeched overhead. Kyla glanced upward and glimpsed the bird before he dipped out of sight between the trees.

She inhaled and exhaled evenly. Peace. Quiet. Nature. She couldn't have asked for anything better. Maybe she'd take Thor on a run every morning before lunch this week.

Kyla wiped a hand across her damp forehead. Maybe not.

A bird chirped and fled as Thor lunged for it. Kyla tugged him around to the front of the house, deciding to take a shower and a nap and worry about lunch later.

However, as the driveway came into view, she spotted a blue Jeep parked behind her Beetle. She froze, and a shiver crawled up her spine.

Alan drove a black car. It wasn't him. Someone was here,

though, unless the place had a shared driveway or something. Kyla shook her head and took a deep breath, then led Thor up the porch stairs. The door was locked. Her breath whooshed out in relief. No one was here—she was just being paranoid. She needed to relax and stop jumping every time leaves rustled. Thor pranced next to her, anxious to be off his leash.

"All right, baby, but you gotta be good." Kyla unlocked the door, then unclipped Thor, allowing him to pelt into the cabin ahead of her.

Assuming he'd head directly for his water bowl, the puppy surprised her and beelined for the stairs. Kyla shrugged and headed for the couch.

In the spot Thor had lain earlier, a red canvas duffle bag now slumped against the leather.

A low, masculine voice rumbled upstairs.

Her pulse leaped into her throat. Neither the bag nor the car was Alan's, but somehow, he'd followed her. On tiptoes, Kyla picked her way into the well-stocked kitchen. There had to be something in this chef's paradise she could use to defend herself.

A glistening, dark wood knife block stood on the counter, and she pulled the largest knife. Though Kyla had no idea if she could use it on someone, she only knew she couldn't possibly make it up those stairs unarmed.

She crept across the living room and up the stairs as quietly as she could manage. At the top, she made out the voice more clearly.

"Okay, settle down," the interloper said with laughter in his voice. Kyla clutched the knife tighter, steadied herself, and stalked the rest of the hall to the bedroom the voice came from.

"Oh."

Crouched on the floor in front of Thor was one of the most handsome men she'd ever seen. He looked up at her with clear, blue eyes, his defined arm muscles rippling as he stopped petting Thor's head. He stood suddenly and ran a hand through his dark, wavy hair. Her mouth went dry as she realized he had almost half a foot on her.

"Don't stab me." He put up his hands, and the dog leaned against his leg. "I'm Josh Hamilton. This is my bedroom." He extended a hand.

Kyla blinked. Josh Hamilton? She peered at him. An old, faded picture from college was on Dylan's fridge, the only picture she'd ever seen of his mysterious brother. Though he'd grown up and filled out, the man standing in front of her was definitely him. She nodded. "I've seen you on Dylan's fridge."

Her grip on the knife loosened. Dylan's brother wouldn't mean her any harm, though he had to be pissed she had taken over his bedroom.

Oh, damn. His bedroom.

"Um, I am so, so sorry." Kyla pressed the knife's handle into his open hand. "I didn't know anyone was going to be here. Dylan said I could come up. I've been dealing with some... drama. I'm just going to grab my stuff and go."

She brushed past him, and Thor trailed after her, but she could only spare him a single pat as she quickly repacked her week-ender. God, she had so much lingerie with her. She'd gone shopping this morning before she left Missoula to replace what Alan had stolen and had planned to do a boudoir shoot by herself to reclaim a little of her confidence, but Josh had to be wondering—

"Rosy, right?" Josh asked.

Kyla turned to look at him, and Josh quickly glanced away from the sky-blue bra in her hand. How did he know that name?

"Uh, Kyla, actually."

Josh frowned. "Okay. If you're not Rosy, then who are you and how the hell did you get the key to my cabin?"

She flushed, feeling silly and exposed. "Well, I am Rosy."

"Do you have multiple personalities?"

Kyla couldn't help herself. She laughed at the sheer ridiculousness of the situation. "Could be, I suppose. It depends on whom you ask." She gestured to underscore her point and realized she still held the blue bra. Josh tracked its progress with his eyes, and she blushed violently before shoving it into the depths of her bag.

"Rosy is Dylan's nickname for me." She bit her lip. She owed Josh an explanation for her presence. "He's my best friend. He gave me the key."

Josh smiled easily. "The nickname suits. How about some lunch?"

Kyla looked over the huge pile of clothes she had to repack and thought about the three-hour drive back home. She'd really better get started.

"It's just lunch," Josh said.

Kyla hesitated.

"Thor likes me." Josh raised a teasing eyebrow.

Right on cue, the dog barked.

She laughed. She really didn't want to hit the road or go back to her ruined apartment. "You've got me there. Okay, I'll take you up on that lunch, thanks."

"I'll go get started." He turned to leave.

Gratitude at the kindness of this virtual stranger overwhelmed Kyla, and she raced after him. "Josh."

He turned back to face her, and the full force of his eyes made the words catch in her throat. She'd never seen eyes quite so blue. "Thank you. For letting me stay."

He shrugged. "I just offered lunch."

Right. Of course. She was an idiot. Her cheeks heated, and she whirled back to her packing. He caught her arm as she turned, and she looked back at him. For a moment, he stared into her eyes, and it felt as if time stopped.

"Now I see why Dylan calls you Rosy," he whispered.

Kyla narrowed her eyes. She couldn't have two Hamilton men making fun of her for blushing. "I hate that nickname."

He shook his head. "No, you don't. But I can come up with my own."

Kyla laughed, surprised to find herself charmed and wondering what nicknames he'd come up with.

"You can stay." He let go of her arm. "I'll take one of the guest rooms."

Gratitude swelled in her again, and before she could think, Kyla lifted onto her tiptoes and pressed a kiss to his stubbled cheek.

He froze.

"Uh, thanks," she murmured before wheeling to unpack once more. Josh's footsteps sounded on the stairs.

Why had she done that?

* * *

Kyla, freshly showered and wrapped in a clean white towel, rooted through the mountain of clothes on the bed. What did a girl wear to an impromptu lunch in a cabin in the woods with her best friend's brother?

An antique rotary phone on the bedside table trilled and made her jump a foot in the air. She picked up the receiver and pressed it to her ear. "Hello?"

"Kyla?"

"Dylan. Oh, my god. You didn't tell me your"—she mentally filled in *sexy as hell*—"brother would be here. How could you?"

He snorted. "Well, seeing as I'm calling you from your cell phone, I couldn't very well get in touch with you, could I?"

She bit her lip. "Oops. I left it on the charger, huh?"

"Yeah. Oops," Dylan said. "I am sorry, though. I didn't know he'd be there until I woke this morning. He left a voicemail."

"Do you think I should just come home? It's his place, right? He said I could stay, but I don't know." Kyla really didn't want to head back to Missoula, not until Dylan texted her a picture of Alan in cuffs.

"He's hiding out from girl trouble, so I wouldn't exactly expect a barrel of laughs. But if he said you can stay, you can stay." Dylan sounded strange, but she couldn't quite put her finger on why.

"Aw, poor guy. At least we can mope together." Kyla cradled the phone with her shoulder and pulled a light blue cotton sundress from the pile. Pretty and comfy. Perfect for this weird situation.

"You need the break." Dylan cleared his throat. "I miss you already, though."

Something in Dylan's tone had Kyla's stomach plummeting. "We're good, right?" It was hard enough to relax with Alan on the loose—she had to know things were okay with Dylan.

He laughed. "You worry too much."

Dylan sounded forced, but the audio quality of the landline could be playing tricks. "Okay. Good."

A beat of silence passed.

"I called to let you know I talked to Alan," Dylan said.

"You talked to him? Already? Oh, god, how bad was it?" Kyla dropped onto the bed, trying not to imagine the worst.

"The fucker slipped something in his desk drawer as I entered his office," Dylan said.

"Do you think it was my...you know?" Kyla couldn't believe Alan would be so cocky as to bring her underwear to work.

"It looked small and dark, maybe rectangular," Dylan said

in his steely cop voice. "I just wanted to let you know we spoke to him in case he tries to reach you when you get back."

"Thanks." Would Alan have the courage to contact her after facing Dylan? Kyla shivered, thankful she'd left her phone in Missoula so she didn't have to find out.

"Look... Alan said he was with Leanne yesterday."

"Leanne? As in his secretary?"

"Yeah. And she confirmed his alibi. Sorry."

Kyla's stomach roiled. A week ago, she would have been devastated just thinking of them together. Now, real fear for Leanne's safety took precedence. "No, no. Alan and I have been apart for long enough now. I can handle hearing about them."

"I'm proud of you," Dylan said.

"Why didn't you arrest him, though? I mean, it's more than obvious he's the vandal. And thief. And all-round nuisance."

"I know it's him, you know it's him, but he has an alibi. I have to do this by the book, Rosy. I don't want him slipping through the cracks."

"I know, I know." She cleared her throat and tried not to think about the roughness in his voice. "Okay. I'm hanging up."

"Love you, girl."

"Love you more."

She replaced the phone on the receiver and released a deep, cleansing breath. She did love Dylan. Even talking to him made her feel better. She had never noticed until Alan called her out, but she and Dylan clicked from the beginning and never looked back.

Kyla could take this time away to relax because she knew Dylan would find evidence to arrest Alan. He always had her back. All she had to worry about was a week in the woods with the other handsome Hamilton brother.

CHAPTER FOUR

Josh. A little. He hadn't planned to cook for two, but when he unloaded his groceries in the kitchen, he found the cupboards and fridge full. Kyla had brought enough food for weeks, so he figured she wouldn't mind if he prepared it for them.

He didn't often bring women up here. It still felt enough like his mom's cabin to be sacred. Had he known Tasha was the kind of woman she'd turned out to be, he would never have planned to share this part of his heart and soul with her. He'd been trying to... He didn't know. Compensate for all the times he hadn't been there for her? Regardless, it hadn't been enough.

He stopped stirring. Fuck, he'd given Tasha directions to the place. She wouldn't dare show up, would she? He didn't think so. Tasha hated being wrong, and she was really wrong this time.

Josh minced a chili pepper, the secret ingredient that made everyone go wild for his marinara sauce. He stirred the pepper into the sauce and wiped his forehead with the back of his arm, careful not to touch his eyes.

He was done trying to find "the one." Romance only complicated his life, and he had the bakery to focus on. He certainly wasn't going to compromise on his dreams just to have someone in his bed at night, not even the unexpectedly sexy woman stuck in his cabin with him.

He couldn't stop thinking about how the bright pink sports bra had clung to her curves, the way her chocolate brown hair curled messily over her forehead, how she'd put Tasha's magazine-ready looks to shame without an ounce of makeup.

Josh stirred the sauce once more, washed his hands, then pulled his phone from his pocket. He hadn't wanted to turn it on but wondered if Romeo was all right at the bakery. Once the phone loaded, he checked his calls and grimaced. Seventeen missed calls from Natasha. Three from Dylan. Nothing from the bakery. That was a relief, at least.

His phone vibrated in his hand with an incoming call, and though tempted to shut it off, he caught sight of Dylan's name on the screen. His eyebrows shot up. Dylan never called him, only texted. He accepted the call quickly and put it on speaker.

"Hey, Dylan. Is everything okay?" Josh cleared his throat. He didn't expect to be emotional over an actual phone call from his brother, but he was.

"Your lovely ex called me," Dylan replied.

Ah, not a brotherly call. A complaint. "Damn it."

"How the hell did she get my number?" Dylan asked.

Josh sighed. "A few months back, I got into a fender bender. She demanded some kind of emergency number, and I... couldn't come up with another option. Sorry."

"She's whiny as hell. I hung up pretty quick."

"Sounds like her." Josh rolled his neck. Though the conversation wasn't what he'd hoped for, it was something, at least. "Just ignore her calls, okay?"

"Consider it done. I've ignored the last five." Dylan cleared his throat. "So, have you spoken to Kyla?"

Josh glanced at the stairs. "Briefly, but she's in the shower."

Dylan paused. "Joshua, if you—"

"Don't worry so much." Josh sprinkled salt into the bubbling sauce. He knew the drill. Any woman in Dylan's orbit stayed out of Josh's. "Her virtue is safe."

"I'm not messing around." Dylan's voice dropped even lower. "We're not doing this again."

"I *won't*. But she almost killed me with my nice butcher knife. Why the hell is she here?" Josh took two steps to the cabinet and grabbed one of the three boxes of pasta Kyla had brought.

"I tried to call you both, but your phone went straight to voicemail, and she left hers at home. Her ex is threatening her. I sent her up there for her safety, and I needed the space for my investigation."

Josh strode back to the stove and stirred his sauce before putting the pasta in a pot of boiling water. "Jeez, all right. There's no way I'm kicking her out now. Should I keep an eye out for anyone?"

"I doubt he'll find her up there." Dylan sighed heavily. "But her ex isn't taking the news she doesn't want him back very well. I'm hoping he never even knows she left. Please look out for her, Josh."

Josh leaned against the counter and rolled his eyes. Dylan always worried too much. "I'll make sure to lock the cabin door."

"She's a big part of my life. I'm sure I don't need to remind you about Sky—"

"I get it! I'm picking up what you're putting down. I'm not dumb, and you don't need to treat me like I am," Josh snapped.

He didn't think of himself as an angry guy, but between Tasha and finding a stranger in his cabin, he was at his breaking point. Dylan fell silent for a moment, seemingly considering what Josh said. Josh took a few deep breaths and stirred the sauce again.

"All right. I hear you," Dylan said. "This might be a good chance to prove you've grown up."

"Yeah, okay," Josh muttered. He didn't like feeling chided. "Later."

"Later."

Josh ended the call and slipped his phone into his pocket as soft footfalls sounded on the staircase. Excitement shot through him, but he knew he had to tamp it down. He didn't want that to be the last time he spoke to his brother.

CHAPTER FIVE

The aroma of warm basil and oregano drifted up the stairs as Kyla padded down the stairs with an armful of Malinois. Thor was getting too big to be carried, but she needed the support to face Josh again.

She'd wanted to be embarrassed he had seen her underwear. Instead, she'd found herself wildly turned on and decided to slip into the sky-blue lingerie set Josh had noticed. She didn't plan on showing it to him again—Kyla was hardly the one-night-stand type, and Josh would be too messy a choice for that anyway—but she could really use the confidence boost the lingerie gave her. She'd then put on the dress she picked out and left her hair damp and wavy. Kyla was too hungry to waste time with the blow dryer and hair straightener.

She smoothed her hand over Thor's back and headed to the kitchen for what smelled like a fabulous meal. A man had never cooked for her before. Ever. Not her father, her ex-fiancé, or, hell, even Dylan.

Josh was as sexy from behind as he was from the front: broad shoulders, tight ass, and strong legs. He stood at the stove with a white dish towel thrown over his shoulder in a gray T-shirt and basketball shorts. He tapped his foot to the beat of the jazz music, which played from a small stereo on the counter. She kissed Thor between his velvety ears and took a shuddering breath.

"Hey," Kyla said.

"Hey." Josh glanced at her. She didn't think she imagined the heat in his gaze, but he turned quickly back to something on the burner. "You know the dog can walk, right?"

"Yeah, yeah." Kyla settled Thor on his large dog bed, which Josh must have moved to the den, then drifted back to the kitchen. She sat on a leather stool at the kitchen island. That way, she could block her view of his ass and maybe have a reasonable conversation with the man. The faded photo on Dylan's refrigerator in Missoula really hadn't done Josh justice. "Everything looks great," she said, her voice coming out much huskier than intended. Her face grew hot. "That sounded like a pickup line. I'm sorry."

"No need to apologize," Josh replied, seemingly trying to contain a grin.

"Everything looks great?" Kyla dropped her face into her hands, but not before she caught a glimpse of the smile that broke across his face. He had dimples. Life truly was unfair. "I may as well have said, call the cops because it's illegal to look that good."

He coughed out a laugh. "Okay, I have to know where your mind is going."

She recognized the lilt of mirth in his voice, and as she peeked between her fingers, he turned to face her for the first time since she entered the room. The full weight of his attention was almost too much to bear.

"God. Never mind. You know what? I'm just gonna go back upstairs." She uncovered her flaming face to push herself up from her chair, but her elbows almost gave out when he turned a concentrated gaze on her.

"Can I come with?"

For a moment, he seemed deadly serious, and she found herself on the verge of a tremulous *yes*. From the intensity in his eyes, if she did, the cabin could burn down around them, and she wouldn't notice. Then, the same brilliant grin broke across his face, and he winked as he turned back to whatever bubbled on the stove.

"Now that's good flirting." She tried to catch her breath and keep her tone light. They were just joking around as friends would. He laid down the spoon and started rustling through the fridge. She tracked his progress through the kitchen. Friends.

"Really? I thought it was pretty damn forward," Josh said. She caught something new in his voice, but he smiled when he turned back with a few bundles of herbs in his muscular arms.

"But I would imagine it works, though, right? Like, a girl would know you were into her."

"You tell me." Josh quirked a smile as he set up another cutting board across the island from her. His hands moved with a practiced deftness she couldn't help but admire. She very carefully kept her mind away from other things that deftness could be useful for. Mostly.

"See, you are good at this." She giggled as she leaned comfortably back in her chair.

"I seem to have lost my touch," he muttered under his breath. Kyla almost missed the moment when he laid down the knife and reached for her hand, but she clearly saw when he pulled back. The air between them crackled, and her breath caught in her throat. Josh picked up the cutting board and carried it back to the stove, not making eye contact with her as he stirred the freshly chopped greenery into the sauce. The atmosphere in the cabin seemed to have dropped five degrees. Even Thor quirked an ear as if he could sense the change.

"Oh, god, were you flirting with me just now?" Kyla tried to smirk and give Josh a chance to deflect, but her question was all too genuine. His shoulders heaved with his deep breath. If he rejected her, she could always go home.

"If you have to ask." He spun to face her with a hand on his heart and a wounded expression. His apron flared with the turn, and they both slumped on the island in helpless giggles.

She couldn't remember the last time she laughed like this with anyone but Dylan. She was wiping tears from her eyes when his face settled into something a little more serious.

"Kyla, what I said earlier about going upstairs—" A rattling lid indicated a pot on the stove was close to bubbling over. Josh quickly removed the sauce from its burner. His butt even looked good as he saved lunch. Josh turned back faster than she expected, but his smile didn't seem as if he'd caught her looking. "You know, I'm ordinarily a better cook than this."

"I believe you." Kyla held up her hands. Josh laughed, and it did funny things to her heart.

"Maybe it's the testosterone talking, but I don't want you to just believe me. I want to prove it to you."

Kyla didn't think she imagined the honesty in his voice.

"That's not very common," she said bitterly, then winced. If she couldn't keep her inside thoughts inside, she would never survive this trip.

"What isn't?"

"Sharing your, uh, desires." She bit her lip. Josh didn't need to hear about her trust issues over lunch.

"Oh, honey. You would know if I had shared my desires," he said with a goofy grin as he piled pasta onto plates.

"Now you're keeping secrets? Not a great way to make a first impression, Mr. Hamilton." Kyla watched as Josh's face dimpled once more, the joking smile becoming genuine. It was a transition she could get used to.

"Lunch is served, Ms. Rosy." He carried the finished plates to the island. "Or is it Ms. Kyla, of no given last name? I'm having trouble keeping all your aliases straight." Josh winked as he took the seat next to her.

"Aliases?" Kyla raised an eyebrow. "You think I'm a criminal? Here to steal what, exactly?"

The romantic in Kyla hoped he'd say something poetic like "his heart." Instead, he glanced around quickly and said, "My incredible DVD collection?"

"It is incredible. *The Creature from the Black Lagoon* is my favorite." Kyla took a bite of her lunch. The rich flavors spread over her palate, followed by a kick of heat. "Mm, this is delicious."

"I'm glad you approve. Have I impressed you yet?"

"Very much so. Is this your recipe?" she asked in the small gap between bites.

"My mom's, actually, but I tweaked it a little," Josh said. She couldn't help but notice how his whole body relaxed when they talked about cooking. "I used some of the groceries you bought. Sorry. Probably should've asked first."

"No problem." She met his sheepish smile with one of her own. "If you're this good in the kitchen, I can't imagine how good you are..." Kyla's face flushed again. She quickly shoveled in another bite of pasta as though it would distract him, but Josh had no mercy.

"In the bedroom? See, you're doing all right with the flirting." His knee bumped into hers under the counter, and he quickly moved it away. Kyla savored the brief brush of warm skin, realizing her skirt had snagged on the stool and crept almost halfway up her thighs. She fixed it when he looked down at his lunch.

She had fun joking around with Josh. It was clear he liked to laugh and didn't take life too seriously, the exact opposite of Alan.

Then, Thor suddenly rocketed out of bed to bark at a squirrel outside, and Kyla remembered how he did the same thing at the window in Dylan's living room while they watched TV together. She shivered at the memory of her ruined apartment back in Missoula.

"What's wrong?" he asked when she fell silent. His eyebrows knit together with concern, and her heart melted so much she almost blurted everything out. Instead, she took a steadying breath.

"It's nothing, really." Kyla ate a casual bite of pasta. Well, it was supposed to be casual. If the amused smile on Josh's face was anything to go by, she hadn't quite pulled it off.

"Don't take this the wrong way"—he pointed his fork at her —"but you are horrible at hiding your feelings."

She narrowed her eyes and pointedly ignored the telltale burn on her cheeks. "Okay, smarty pants. If it's so obvious, what am I thinking?"

"You're thinking…" He paused as if deep in thought. "Shut up, Josh?" His posture was all comedy, but Kyla could read the genuine concern in his question. If she said yes, he'd leave her be. She didn't want to be alone with her thoughts, but she didn't want to explain them either.

Deciding to shift attention to Josh, Kyla shook her head. "Dylan told me you were in a relationship and—"

He held up his hands. "Say no more. I've been a single man for"—he looked at his watch—"eighteen hours. No, make that eighteen and a half. She wasn't the faithful sort."

"I'm sorry." Kyla covered his large, callused hand with hers. She didn't want to ever let go.

"I'm not, Kyla." Josh left his hand there for a moment. The

silence stretched between them, and he looked at her like he wanted to say something important. Then, he snatched his hand back, ran it through his hair, and started moving dishes to the sink. Kyla's heart sank. She'd crossed a boundary, obviously, but that didn't stop her wish Josh would stop cleaning and wrap his strong arms around her.

"Well, if it's any consolation, I know how it feels when someone cheats on you."

"If I need a hug, you'll be my first ask," he answered a little too quickly.

Kyla tried to remind herself Josh was doing the right thing by ignoring their attraction and that even a few nights together would be too complicated. Regardless, she enjoyed his presence here. He was a great chef, a good comedian, and showed signs of being an amazing friend. A trip to the woods had seemed like such a good idea when Dylan suggested it. Now, she knew she never could have survived this week all by herself.

She just wished he'd stop flirting with her because, even if he did so jokingly, it made doing the right thing feel so wrong.

CHAPTER SIX

Josh set the last of the clean plates back in the cupboard as Kyla rinsed out the sink. He had argued, but Kyla insisted on washing the lunch dishes. This girl was everything Tasha wasn't. Shy, but funny and a little pushy at the same time. She actually seemed interested in *him*. He wasn't conceited, but every man needed his ego stroked occasionally.

Josh hadn't felt this carefree in a long time. Six months, to be exact. When he thought about it, he realized he'd always felt on edge with Tasha. He never really knew what she wanted or what would set her off on her next rant, and his efforts to please her often went unappreciated. She always wanted things he wasn't willing or able to give.

With Kyla... Josh sighed. With Kyla, there were too many obstacles in his way. He hadn't been single twenty-four hours yet, and Dylan had been pretty clear on the phone. Josh kept telling himself that, but every time she blushed...

"So, how long are you planning to stay?" He leaned against the counter and watched her. Kyla's cheeks flushed a little under his gaze, and the tip of her tongue peeked out to wet her lips. She dried her hands on a dish towel, then folded it into a neat little square. Damn, she was cute.

"That's really up to you, seeing as I'm crashing your solo vacation."

He smiled, something that came easy around this woman. "You're welcome to stay as long as you'd like."

"I was originally planning to stay a week. I have a wedding to shoot this coming weekend. I need to be back in Missoula the day before to check gear, charge batteries, and clear memory cards." Kyla shrugged. "The couple I'm shooting is the cutest, and their venue is to die for. Maryanne's dad is a sculptor and designed their wedding arch. Once they get flowers on it"—she grinned—"let's just say, their photos are going to be incredible. I'm pretty excited."

She seemed passionate about her work, and he admired that. Josh felt the same way about the bakery. He lived and breathed it. In fact, his entire world revolved around the business. It was satisfying to meet someone with that same drive, that same desire to succeed at something she loved. More than satisfying. A fucking turn-on.

"But if you want me out sooner, I can leave."

Now that he'd gotten past his initial annoyance and spent time with her, he wanted nothing more than to get to know her.

"No. Stay." Josh crossed his arms over his chest. He didn't miss how her gaze flicked to his flexed biceps. "Any plans for this afternoon?"

"Honestly, I had planned to just sit by the water and do absolutely nothing."

"That sounds awesome. Want some company, or do you need some time alone?"

A moment of silence passed. An echo of the hurt when he'd pulled his hand away played across her face again. Josh mentally kicked himself. The last thing he wanted was to lead her on when he couldn't do anything.

"I wouldn't mind the company," she said slowly.

"Great. I'll grab a couple of chairs and some beer, and we can head down there." That was a perfectly normal, friendly activity.

* * *

Josh traipsed alongside Kyla on the rocky lakeshore. Thor tugged on the leash, anxious to get to the water.

"It's gorgeous here," she said.

"It's heaven on earth," Josh agreed. He had loved the reflection of the mountains on the lake for as long as he could remember. When they reached the perfect spot, Josh set the six-pack of beer down in the ice-cold water and laughed as Thor tentatively stepped into the glacial lake. "Cold, buddy?"

Thor ran over to him and jumped up on his chest, soaking his T-shirt.

"God, I'm sorry," Kyla said, trying to yank Thor back.

"Don't worry about it." He set up their chairs on either side of the six-pack. "I'm on vacation. Nothing is going to bother me."

Kyla laid down a towel for the dog behind them and set a large chew on top of it. He could tell by Thor's tail they were both about to have a great afternoon.

Kyla sat down, closed her moss-green eyes, and turned her pretty face toward the sun's heat. He tried not to notice the long line of her neck or the tiny birthmark on her collarbone. God, he needed a cold shower.

"This is the life."

Josh opened a beer and hummed. "No kidding. Just to have

a chance to sit down without thinking about work is pretty novel."

"Dylan told me you have a bakery." Kyla opened her eyes.

"Yeah." He weighed his next words carefully. "I wanted to honor my mom."

Kyla nodded slowly. It was clear she didn't want to push, but he wanted to tell her. Was that a friendly impulse? With her ex threatening her, she didn't need more trouble in her life—all she needed was a friend. The longer he spent with her, the harder it was to remember.

"We had a bake sale at school one year. I worked hard with her over cookies the entire night before, and mine sold out before anyone else's." He grinned, remembering the pride on his mom's face when he told her. "It's one of my best childhood memories."

Kyla smiled back. "Competitive much?"

"A bit, yeah." He laughed. "But honestly, I think it helps. I got the business in the black so quickly because I didn't want to lose."

She stared out over the lake, and he wondered how the view looked to her photographer's eye. Beautiful, he hoped.

"So, why do you do it?" he asked. She cocked an eyebrow at him. "Photography, I mean."

"I think...it's really easy to forget special things," she said after a little while. "Or, I guess, to forget things can be special. Photography is a way to capture something special, unique, and be able to view it later. That's why I love photographing weddings. Life is messy and often boring, relationships doubly so, and I think it's important to have fairy-tale moments to fall back on. To remember the world can be beautiful." She set her beer aside and drew her knees to her chest. The blue fabric of her dress bunched up to expose slim, pale thighs. Josh wanted to gather her in his arms and kiss away the creases that formed on her forehead. He wanted to spin fairy tales for her to remember. He wanted—

He wanted his brother to speak to him without that hard edge in his voice. Josh had almost forgotten what the real Dylan sounded like. Unbidden, Josh remembered a moment at this same lakeside years ago. He and Dylan had begged, pleaded, and wheedled until their parents had finally caved and gotten them the biggest, most ridiculous water guns they'd ever seen. Then, they'd spent days building ramparts and shelters out of the lakeshore rocks. The two of them staged the greatest water-gun fight this national park had ever seen, which ended in a glorious stalemate. He could still hear their laughter bouncing off the mountains.

Josh took a pull of his beer and nodded. He had to defuse the moment. "So, you have the week off most of the time?" Stupid.

"Um, yeah." Kyla seemed to snap out of her trance. She rearranged her dress primly over her knees. "People rarely marry during the work week, but I have to edit my photos from the previous weekend. This week I'm taking some example shots for a workshop I do. I…haven't had time. Someone broke into my apartment."

Josh almost choked on his beer. Dylan had really undersold the problem. He swallowed heavily. "That's awful. You lose anything valuable?"

Kyla blushed. "Just my underwear."

Josh's eyebrows rose. "Really? So it's a pervert, not a thief?"

"Well, technically, it's both. And a vandal." Kyla jutted out her chin, and Josh realized he'd hit a sorer spot than he realized. "I'm certain it's my ex. Dylan just can't prove it. Yet."

"Shit," Josh said, unable to help himself. "So you date the crazy type too?" As soon as the words were out in the air, he wished he could take them back. At least he wouldn't have to worry about his attraction to Kyla if he kept making such an ass of himself.

During the half-second of silence that followed, Josh seriously considered throwing himself into the lake. Then, Kyla let out a sharp bark of laughter and buried her head in her hands.

"I guess I do," she said. "I found him cheating on me with his secretary, and I ended my relationship. Alan wants me back, though. He left a note on my car to that effect yesterday." Her shoulders shook, which could have been from laughter or tears. Josh felt the same protective impulse as his brother and tried to smother it. Clearly Kyla had enough over-interested men to worry about.

"What an ass," he said lamely. "For cheating and for not letting you go. Though I can imagine he regrets losing you."

Kyla looked up at him, face red and eyes helpless. "You just met me."

He tried a jokey grin, but the moment weighed it down. He ended up staring into her eyes. "I'm a great judge of character." That was why he'd do everything in his power not to hurt her.

CHAPTER SEVEN

Kyla led the way up the stairs to bed. She glanced over her shoulder. "Thank you for today. The beer, the amazing dinner, and the movie..."

"Of course." Josh smiled. She wished his dimples didn't make her weak in the knees. "I didn't think I wanted company, but I have to admit, today was good. Really, I should be thanking you."

Heat rose on her cheeks. She'd thought the same as she ate his homemade pizza, sipped a glass of white wine, and stole glimpses of him while vintage horror played on the TV. Kyla wished the jump-scares still worked on her so she could've leaped to him for protection. Or at least trusted her acting skills enough to lie. Instead, they'd kept a perfectly respectable distance between them on the huge couch.

"Are you sure you're okay in the guest room?"

"Is that an invite?" he asked, then laughed. She stumbled very slightly, and he caught her shoulder with his large hand. "I'm teasing. Yes, the guest room is great."

She met his gaze, and he lingered for just a beat longer than he should have. Kyla's cheeks warmed further, and she started to lean in.

Thor barked sharply. Right. She leaned down to stroke the dog's ears and dispel the tension. "Okay, then. Goodnight."

He blinked, smiled a little too widely, and nodded. "Right. Yeah. Goodnight, Kyla."

When he disappeared behind the guestroom door, Kyla leaned against the wall and sighed. If Josh didn't stop looking at her like that, she would really start to get the wrong idea.

She settled into the master bedroom. Thor instantly passed out on the foot of the bed, but in case he wanted to roam, she left the door open a crack. Then, on a whim, she put on her sheerest nightgown to sleep.

Kyla expected to be up all night daydreaming about Josh or worrying about Alan, but the fresh mountain air soothed her racing mind.

* * *

KYLA WOKE UP WITH THE WARMTH OF THE SUN ON HER FACE. SHE pulled the soft comforter up to her chin and cuddled back into the mountain of pillows on Josh's bed. If this counted as roughing it, she'd plan to come up to the mountains more often.

To Josh's cabin, that was. When he was here. Spending time with the man had been...interesting. He acted just as sweet and caring as Dylan, but it wasn't at all the same. Dylan flirted, sure, but she loved him like a brother. Josh, however, had an undeniable sexual quality that set her nerves alight. She wouldn't have minded if he'd taken her hand and dragged her to bed to make slow love to her, yet he never made a move except for simple yet sensual touches that left her craving something he hadn't even put on offer. Or had, for a moment, before he took it back. She only wished she knew why.

She punched her pillow. An immensely powerful man, that Josh Hamilton.

Kyla sat up and looked around the room. She had woken up alone. Where the hell did the dog go? She pulled on a pair of yoga pants and a sweatshirt, then braided her hair before venturing out of the bedroom.

She passed the guestroom. The door was open, bed made. She caught a whiff of cinnamon and hurried downstairs. A pan of fresh-baked cinnamon rolls sat on a trivet on the island, one missing from the corner. A note lay beside it.

Kyla, enjoy breakfast. I took Thor with me on a hike. I hope the peace and quiet helps.

XX Josh

"You're perfect," she said with a sigh.

Kyla cut herself a still-warm cinnamon roll, poured a cup of coffee from the half-pot Josh had left behind, and took them upstairs. Breakfast in bed. She could get used to this life.

Unfortunately, work awaited. She opened her laptop and started uploading the unedited photos from the past weekend.

It was impossible not to moan when she took a bite of the cinnamon roll. The dough tasted light and sweet, balanced perfectly by the tang of the frosting. "God, that's good." She needed to start all her days at Josh's bakery. Her waistband and bank account would suffer, but the eye candy made it all worth it.

While she waited for her photos to load, she checked her e-mail. New gig, new gig, spam, and Dylan.

Rosy.

Taking the chance you're on your laptop because you're always on your laptop. I just wanted to tell you I miss you, and I'm not thinking about the kiss at all.

Love you, Dylan.

"GOD, DYLAN. WHY ARE YOU MAKING THIS WEIRD?"

Kyla fell back on her pillows, Josh's pillows, and sighed. When she closed her eyes, she could feel Dylan's lips against hers. Soft but strong, unyielding. She could have leaned into the kiss. She could've let the night end differently, but she hadn't. She'd pulled back, and if she were being honest, she'd make the same choice again, especially knowing she'd end up at a gorgeous cabin in the woods with a gorgeous man.

Kyla snagged her coffee mug off the bedside table and took a sip. She had to respond to Dylan.

I AM ON MY LAPTOP BECAUSE I HAVE WORK TO DO. ANY LUCK WITH THE B&E?

SHE CLOSED HER E-MAIL BEFORE HE COULD RESPOND AND TOOK another bite of the cinnamon roll. She didn't want to talk to Dylan about the kiss. She wanted to talk to Josh.

Guilt twisted up her insides like a pretzel. She knew the rules about friends and siblings. She needed to lay off.

She had only met Josh yesterday, but it felt as if the stars had aligned. They'd talked for hours at the lake while they watched Thor play in the water. This morning, Josh knew she needed time to work, so he took the puppy and left her alone. No guy had ever been that thoughtful.

The reasons not to act on her attraction to Josh stacked up like the cordwood piled outside. He was her best friend's brother. He'd ended a relationship barely over a day ago. He'd been cheated on. No matter how much he reassured her, no one could take that in stride. Unfortunately, she knew that firsthand.

She wanted to kiss him. To hear him laugh. To find out how his hands felt on her skin and his body against hers.

At a small *ding*, Kyla realized her photos had uploaded. Work waited for no hunky brothers. She turned on an audiobook, hoping the background noise would keep her out of a mental labyrinth.

She reviewed shot after brilliant shot of the weekend's wedding, editing the light and blurring the background so her bride and groom were the focus of each image. Kyla relived the beautiful moments, and a soft smile stretched over her face. At least somebody's life was easy right now.

After an hour, Kyla stood up to stretch. The photos had turned out brilliantly. She couldn't wait to send a few teasers to the happy couple this week.

The digital clock on her laptop reminded her lunchtime approached, and she hadn't dressed yet. Kyla took a shower and got ready for the day, this time in a pair of coral cotton shorts and a dusty blue T-shirt.

She had just pulled her hair into a messy bun when the front door squeaked open. A little jolt of excitement surged through her at the thought of seeing Josh again. As friends, she reminded herself. Only friends.

Still, Kyla hurried from the master bedroom. She met Thor, pelting up the stairs to greet her. His tongue lolled out the side of his mouth, and his tail wagged. "Hi, baby boy. Look at you. Are you tired?"

She couldn't help but smile at Josh's heavy footsteps on the stairs. She had missed him. "Hey," she said while crouched to stroke Thor's ears.

"Hey. How was your morning?"

Kyla looked up and realized what he wore. Or didn't. His bare chest gleamed with sweat, and basketball shorts clung to his body in all the right places.

She swallowed hard. "Uh. Good. I managed to get a lot of work done." She stood so she could better take in his physique. "I was just heading down for another cinnamon roll, but now I feel guilty."

Josh laughed and ran his hand through his sweaty hair. She wished she could do the same. "Why? Because I came home too soon?"

"No." She gestured to his naked chest, grateful for the reason to stare. "That's why."

He looked down at his perfectly toned body and choked out a laugh. "Life's too short. Eat the pastry. I baked them for you to enjoy."

"If you join me, I'll feel better."

He nodded. "For sure. I'm just going to shower, and I'll be right down."

Kyla bit her lip as she imagined what the streams of water cascading down his naked chest might look like, where they might lead. As she finally dragged her gaze away from the expanse of skin, she caught Josh staring at her. He quirked an inquisitive grin. She could do nothing but laugh and sweep past him, Thor on her heels.

CHAPTER EIGHT

"I'M SERIOUS, KYLA." JOSH DREW A CROSS OVER HIS HEART WITH A finger, then took a large bite of his second cinnamon roll. They sat at the kitchen island, finishing off the pan of buns and calling it lunch. It had been his idea, but Kyla deemed it genius.

His body ached. Thor had gotten exhausted at the top of the mountain, and he'd had to carry the growing puppy most of the way down. When he'd gotten back to the cabin, he'd wanted nothing more than to collapse on the couch and nap the day away.

The more time he spent with Kyla, though, he realized he wouldn't be able to close his eyes if he wanted to. He didn't want to miss a moment of her witty banter or flushed excitement.

Dylan might have warned him off Kyla, but that didn't mean he couldn't look.

"You kissed a man?" Kyla couldn't seem to stop giggling, and he didn't want her to. He only wished she wouldn't duck her head when she did. Already a beautiful woman, but when she laughed, she took his breath away.

He needed to snap out of it. Or go rub one out so he could settle the hell down.

Josh nodded. "I did. It was at a concert, and it was dark."

Kyla ran the tip of her finger through the remaining frosting on her plate and sucked at it. Lucky damn fingertip. "You couldn't tell?" she asked, oblivious to the effect she had on him.

Josh cleared his throat. "No. In my defense, the guy was dressed like a girl. A stunning girl, at that."

"Were you drunk?"

Josh laughed. "I might have imbibed a little."

"Was he a good kisser, at least?"

He ran his fingers through his hair. "Oh, yeah. Best kiss of my life to date."

His confession rewarded him with more bell-like laughter, which ended in a snort. Perfection.

"At least you're honest about enjoying it."

Josh shrugged. "Oh, and that's a secret, by the way. No one knows about that kiss."

"Not even Dylan?" She raised a brow.

"Especially not Dylan."

She rubbed her hands together conspiratorially. "Good to know."

He raised a brow to match her. "Planning on blackmailing me?"

"A person never knows when they'll need such valuable information."

Josh set down his fork and placed his hands on his belly. "God, I'm full."

She met his gaze. "You look exhausted."

"What are you talking about?" he asked through a yawn. "I'm young and fit. Hell, I could go for another hike."

"Mm, yeah, I don't believe you."

"You haven't told me one of your secrets yet. I can't let you get away with that. Not after the kiss story."

Her glance flickered from his eyes to his lips when he said *kiss*. And fuck if he could stop thinking about her mouth. He'd bet money she could top the kiss at the concert.

"I don't know. I've lived a very tame life." She flushed, though. He would have given anything to know what she thought about. Was it a kiss that turned her on? A wild night of sex? Or, better yet, a fantasy?

"You don't have to tell me." He stood up, then winked. "Yet."

She laughed again. "I'll think of something."

Josh hobbled over to the sofa where Thor slept soundly and sat, dropping his head back and closing his eyes. "I must be out of shape."

He opened one eye at Kyla's laugh. She sauntered over to the sofa and sat between the dog and him. Was that a little closer than last night? Was he reading too much into the hand she lay on the cushion between them?

"You're not out of shape at all. God. You're like a masterpiece."

He laughed out of shock. He had noticed her noticing but didn't think she would ever share her thoughts. "Oh, really? You like what you see, huh?"

"I might." She tucked her legs under her ass. Her knee brushed his thigh. Definitely closer. "Sorry."

She didn't move to reposition again. Josh prayed his shorts were thick enough to disguise what this closeness did to him. Maybe another shower was in order.

"Close your eyes," she said.

He sat up. "Why?"

She laughed and shoved his shoulder. "Close them, or I won't tell you my secret, which also happens to be my most embarrassing moment."

"Ha. Okay." He struggled to give up even a moment of looking at her, but he wanted to know, and he had become as attracted to her husky voice as her perfect face or sexy body.

"The first time I saw a penis—"

Josh laughed. "Oh, god."

"Don't laugh."

"Sorry." He opened his eyes to see her face and neck flaming red. "Why are you so embarrassed?"

"I cried."

He quirked a brow. "Really? What did the guy say?"

"He panicked. Drove me home. Never asked me out again."

Josh laughed even harder. "Are you still traumatized?"

She bit her lip. "I've moved on."

"Good to know." He grinned at her. "What made you cry?"

"It moved."

Josh covered his face, trying to hold back his laughter, but he couldn't. She started laughing with him. Her body moved closer to his, her hand on his shaking shoulder.

When he finally caught his breath, he said, "That's a good one, Kyla. Damaged the kid's pride, though. I can guarantee it."

"He'll survive." She shrugged. "In my defense, I wasn't anticipating it. He just whipped it out in the car."

Josh rolled his eyes. "What an ass."

"Assholes aren't all that rare in my experience."

"Yeah? Thinking about anyone in particular?"

"Aren't you supposed to be having a nap?" she asked.

Josh shook his head. "Nah. You're too much fun."

She reached over to scratch Thor's ears. The dog sighed and rolled over, still asleep.

"My ex and I were engaged. Had been for months. I still have the big white dress in my closet." She sighed, clearly trying to look irritated, but Josh thought he saw a sparkle of tears. "I thought I would finally have the wedding I had always dreamed of. But he fell in lust with his secretary."

Her hand lay on her knee. It would be so easy to take it, to offer some support, but he didn't want to interrupt. This trip was supposed to be good for her, too. And he wasn't totally sure where the line between friends and something more lay anymore.

"I was gutted. But now he's gone, I don't have to deal with his anal-retentive behavior, clipped comments, or stifling presence..." She bit her lip and looked up at the ceiling, and for a second, he thought she would burst into tears. Then, she met his eye and unleashed a brilliant smile. "God, it's freeing. And you know, it feels good to say it out loud. To own what happened."

Josh thought about reaching for her hand now, but Dylan's voice sounded in the back of his mind. He patted Kyla on the shoulder before he could stop himself and tried not to wince. "That sounds bad, but also maybe like you dodged a bullet? Save the pretty dress for someone who deserves you, y'know?"

His buddies would mock him if they could hear this. He'd never sounded more awkward. Luckily, Kyla just laughed.

"You're probably right. The craziest part is, Alan acts like he's done nothing wrong." She dropped her head back on the couch at the sheer audacity. A few strands of hair fell over her face, and he ached to push them aside.

"Jeez, he really is an ass. I'm sorry," Josh said. "Someday you'll find someone you can truly love. Hell, maybe we both will."

She picked her head up and eyed him. "Never been in love?"

He paused. Josh was pretty sure this sort of answer sent girls running for the hills, but he certainly wouldn't follow up her honesty with one of his usual artful dodges.

"I don't think so. I thought I'd loved a lot of girls, including my most recent ex, but to hear you talk... I don't know. Nothing has really hurt like that. I'm angry at being played, but I'm not gutted." Josh rolled his neck. "I hope that doesn't make me a shitty person. But I'm more upset she lied than the fact I lost her, you know?"

Kyla nodded thoughtfully, but she didn't run. Thank god.

"I started getting angry at Alan." She smiled ruefully. He wanted to punch the man who put that pain in her eyes. "He's the only man I've ever loved. Giving your heart to someone is dangerous, and I spent a long time being careful."

Kyla picked at the stitching on the couch. Josh could tell she had more to say, so he let the silence linger. It had been a long time since he'd been okay in someone else's silence.

"My dad cheated on my mom. He was my hero growing up, then one day, he suddenly confessed to a year-long affair. A whole other relationship." She shook her head. "I was fifteen, and I swore up and down that would never happen to me."

"I'm sorry." This time, Josh set his hand on hers. He had to keep his touch friendly. He gave her fingers a squeeze, then started to pull back. When she squeezed his hand in return, he knew he hadn't gone too far. He still let go, though. "What did your mother do when she found out?"

"She stayed."

Josh quirked a brow. "Really?"

She laughed humorlessly. "Yeah. Didn't even ask him to stop seeing the other woman. I left home the minute I turned eighteen."

"So, you don't have much to do with your family?"

She shrugged and looked a little sad. "I talk to my mom on the phone sometimes."

"Give me a chance this week to prove to you that not all men are assholes. Yes, your dad was incredibly selfish, and Alan was only thinking with his—"

"Downstairs head?"

Josh laughed. "Exactly."

Kyla pressed her lips together, but her giggles escaped anyway. "I'm sorry. You're being serious and so sweet, and I'm—"

"Adorable?" He couldn't help himself. Whatever else happened, he couldn't let Kyla put herself down.

"I was going to say immature, but I like your word better." She grinned shyly, peeking up at him from under her lashes.

"Thank you for being honest with me," he said. "I know that isn't easy, especially with someone you just met." He couldn't stop the words, too earnest for the promises he'd made, from spilling out of his mouth.

"It doesn't feel as if we've only just met." She flushed as if she regretted speaking. Her skin would be warm if he took her face in his hands. Soft, too, probably. And her lips—

Fuck. Keeping away from her got harder by the moment.

"Is that because Dylan brags about me all the time?" Josh asked. Dylan, he had to keep away for Dylan. He loved his brother.

Kyla laughed. "Yeah, you come up all the time."

That sounded like a lie, her first since they'd sat down. It struck him then that there might be more between Dylan and her than she had let on. Dylan had been vaguely threatening on the phone, but he hadn't implied anything concrete. Josh pulled back. He didn't know what to say or how to ask, but he knew he couldn't relax until he found out.

"What do you have planned this afternoon?" Josh asked instead. The gulf between them suddenly felt massive. Kyla also leaned back as if she felt the shift.

She shrugged. "Maybe I'll go explore. Take a drive."

"Yeah?" He imagined the wind blowing through her hair, the sun on her face. God, he was in trouble.

Gravel crunched outside, and Josh looked toward the front door. Thor sprang from the sofa and raced over, barking.

"Are you expecting someone?" Kyla asked.

He shook his head. "No, not at all."

Kyla pushed up from the couch and strode toward the door. She peeked out the window, then flattened her body to the wall away from the glass.

"What?" Josh asked. The hair on the back of his neck stood up.

Kyla looked at him, pure dread written all over her face. "It's Alan."

CHAPTER NINE

Josh sprang to his feet and crossed the room to the front door, all signs of exhaustion gone. Kyla's heart pounded in her throat. Alan. Here. Had Dylan slipped up and mentioned something?

Josh's body caged her in as he peered through the window. "I don't see anything. Maybe someone just turned around in the driveway?"

Alan had never shown violent tendencies before. Just disloyal ones.

"No. It was him. I know his car. How did he find me?" Kyla looked up at Josh. He looked down at her, and their gazes met. She didn't want to be on the receiving end of the furious expression on his face, but it softened as he held her gaze. If she had been breathing rather than hyperventilating, there might have been a moment between them.

"Did you tell anyone you're here?" Josh looked back out the window.

"Just Dylan and my friend Andrea. Dylan only talked to Alan after I left, so he couldn't have known I was coming here." Andrea hated Alan even more than Dylan did, so she certainly wouldn't have blabbed.

"Could he be tracking you?" Josh remained close to the window, pressed up against her, big and warm. Safe.

"I left my phone in the city. But he's an accountant," she muttered. He didn't have the skills or know-how to trace her to a remote cabin in the mountain. She tried to steady her breathing.

"Let's go for a drive. We'll cruise around and look for his car."

"He's got a black Lexus LS. It's *beautiful*. You can't miss it." Kyla had spent half her time with Alan hearing about the specs of his beautiful car. She wouldn't forget it until her dying day.

Josh whistled. "That's a pretty damn pricy ride."

Kyla took a small step forward, expecting he would move aside. Instead, he closed his arms around her.

"I won't let him hurt you, all right?" Josh paused. "You're family."

She threaded her arms around his waist, pressed her cheek against his chest, and listened to the steady rhythm of his heartbeat. In the quiet, she matched her breathing to his. Family. Life would be so much easier if she could think of this perfect man as family, but even a hug lit her skin on fire. It took all her willpower not to step in closer, tilt her head up, and make the sort of choice she couldn't take back. No man had ever created this visceral reaction in her before.

Thor whined and nudged at her leg. They both laughed, and Josh stepped away. She didn't pull him back in, which counted as a win at this point.

"What if you're right?" She leaned against the front door. "What if I'm just paranoid?"

"Then you have nothing to worry about. But I know I would feel better if we drove around and looked for him." Josh smiled reassuringly.

She closed her eyes and visualized her ransacked apartment. She opened them. "Am I crazy?"

"I don't know you well enough to say either way."

Her mouth dropped open. Josh chuckled. "I'm teasing. Just trying to make you feel better."

It didn't feel like the time for jokes. "Thanks, I guess."

Josh stepped into her space once more, the heat of his body overcoming her fear and irritation. He rested a hand against the door, leaned down, and murmured, "Of course I don't think you're crazy."

Every nerve ending in Kyla's body burst into flame. Alan be damned. She wanted to stay here with Josh forever. She was just about to wind her arms around him and pull him in when he began leashing the dog.

"Let's take my Jeep," he said. Kyla pouted but followed. Josh locked the door of the cabin behind them and checked it twice, presumably for her benefit. The jimmied lock on her apartment sprang to mind, and she threaded her fingers into Thor's fur for comfort.

They loaded up, then Josh pulled his Jeep onto the narrow lane dotted with cabins. "It's always pretty busy in the summer, even on weekdays, but I know most of the families up here."

"Yeah?" She checked every driveway for Alan's flashy car, barely paying attention.

"The house to the left belongs to an elderly couple, but they don't come up much since Robert had a stroke." He pointed out the window. "This one, two cabins to the right, belongs to my best friends. They're great guys. You would love them." Josh laughed. "God, we had so many adventures when we were kids. We used to sneak out, climb down the trees, and take their dad's boat across the lake. In the middle of the night."

"Yikes." She glanced at him, but he focused on the road, searching. "Did you get in trouble?"

"Not really. Their dad was pretty laidback." Josh smiled. "Still is."

Josh continued to tell stories for the rest of the drive, but Kyla only half listened. His chatter became background noise, more to keep her from falling into a panic again than for her to understand. She appreciated the attempt. After a few turns, she even chuckled at a story about Josh getting a fishhook stuck in Dylan's lip. She had no idea where they were, but she hadn't seen any sign of Alan's car.

"Is this all the cabins?" she asked eventually.

"Nah, there are too many," Josh said. "Anything yet?"

She shook her head. "Maybe it wasn't him after all."

"We'll keep looking, okay?"

She nodded, sat back in her seat, and let out a deep breath. "Thank you. I guess the break-in is affecting me more than I thought."

Josh's hand rested on the gearshift. She could make out a few calluses and old scars and suddenly wished she could take his hand, hold it, discover how those calluses felt against her skin...

"That sucks, Kyla. Really. But I have faith in Dylan. He'll figure this out for you."

She nodded once more. She trusted Dylan. She also trusted Josh, and with both Hamilton brothers as friends, she had very little to worry about. As he pulled the car over to the side of a narrow dirt road, she looked up to tell Josh how safe he made her feel, but he turned his burning gaze to hers, and the words caught in her throat. His mouth opened as if he also had something he needed to say. She leaned in slightly.

"Do you want to call him?" Josh asked. "Dylan?"

Kyla felt like he'd thrown a bucket of cold water on her. She blinked a few times, trying to reorient herself as he pulled his phone from the pocket of his shorts.

Her fingers brushed his as she accepted the phone. "Thanks."

"He might not answer right away. Or at all." Josh stared ahead at the road. "Just keep trying."

Maybe the brothers' relationship was worse than she thought. She dialed Dylan's number. Josh started driving again and turned down another backroad. His gaze remained steadfast on the road. She clutched the phone to her ear as the line connected.

"Josh?" Dylan sounded gruff, almost unfamiliar to Kyla.

"No, it's me."

"Hey, Rosy." She could hear the smile in his voice. "What's going on?"

Kyla looked at Josh. He checked down every driveway they passed and had been for the last half an hour. He was giving up his vacation to help her find a car she couldn't even be sure she saw. The Hamilton men were so good to her, too good. She bit her lip.

"Kyla. What's going on?" Dylan's voice became intense.

"I thought I saw Alan's car in our driveway." She tried to keep the tremble out of her voice but based on the way Josh's attention flicked toward her, she hadn't quite succeeded.

"Okay, don't worry. I'll roll over to his office, then his house. I'll find him, promise."

She nodded. "I know you will. Thanks, Dill Pickle."

Kyla hung up and passed the phone back to Josh. "Thanks."

He smiled at her, sweet and teasing at once. "Dill Pickle? Do I get a cute nickname?"

Kyla took a deep breath. There had been no sign of Alan. Maybe she'd been a little paranoid. Alan had no idea where she was, and even if he did, he wouldn't travel three hours just to steal more lingerie from her suitcase—that was if he even *was* the panty thief. She smiled back at Josh.

"Jaybird?"

He snorted. "Like naked as a jaybird? Is that a request?"

She smirked. "Well, that would count as a distraction."

CHAPTER TEN

THEY'D DRIVEN THROUGH GLACIER FOR ANOTHER HOUR WITHOUT seeing any sign of Alan before Josh headed back to the cabin. The more time had passed, the more Kyla seemed to relax. She'd finally started listening to his stories, and every time he made her smile, it felt like winning a million dollars. By the time they entered the cabin, he had been nearly lightheaded with success.

Dylan hadn't called back yet, though. Kyla checked Josh's phone every few minutes. Leave it to his brother to ruin the mood without even showing up.

Kyla had decided a shower would chase away her lingering blues, so Josh got started on the steaks for dinner. Grilling fell pretty far outside his area of expertise, but he realized he'd do just about anything to impress this girl.

The screen door behind him slid open, and Kyla padded out, her hair still damp. It had started to soak through her T-shirt and—

"Hey," he said, impressed he managed to get the word out without sounding strangled. He turned the steaks and closed the lid.

"Hi." She settled herself in the old rope hammock and

folded her arms under her head. Thor already snoozed on a beach blanket beneath the hammock. A small smile crossed Josh's lips as he turned to face her. Kyla drove him absolutely wild, but he wasn't an animal. He liked seeing her comfortable just as much as he enjoyed ogling her.

The more time he spent with her, the less and less sense it made that he'd never gone for the good girl before. Kyla oozed a frank sweetness that turned him on more than he'd thought possible. He had an innate drive to protect her, to tuck her under his arm and fight off anything and anyone trying to steal her joy. Or steal her away from him.

Like his brother. Josh swallowed. Dylan obviously had feelings for Kyla. Even though she lit up when she talked to him, Josh couldn't tell if she had the same feelings for Dylan as he had for her. However, Josh had made his promises. He wouldn't make the same mistake twice.

"What's going on in that head of yours?" Kyla asked. Josh suddenly realized he'd been staring at her silently for several minutes. He chuckled awkwardly and rubbed the back of his neck.

"Do you want the truth or the socially acceptable lie?" Maybe if she picked truth, he'd tell her the dream he'd had about her lips last night.

Kyla flipped onto her stomach in the hammock, studying him through the netting. "The lie. I can figure out the truth."

Josh puffed out a breath and chose his words carefully. "I'm glad we didn't find your ex."

"You...wanted to find him?" She furrowed her brows adorably as she tried to work out his backward logic.

"I wanted to kick his ass." Josh turned the steaks again. It wasn't a lie, but Alan hardly topped Josh's priority list with Kyla so close.

"I don't know how easy that would be. Alan's not your

typical accountant. He's basically a gym rat." Kyla bit her lip and picked at a knot in the hammock.

Josh's blood started to boil. Of course she felt scared. A guy big enough she needed to warn Josh off... Nothing got under his skin worse than asshole dudes. He rolled his shoulders. He needed to lighten the mood before he got seriously angry.

"Well, everyone knows it's not as much about size as how you use it."

A wicked smirk spread across her face. "Oh yeah? Would you know something about that?"

He spluttered. He meant he could take on her buff ex, but she'd alluded to something completely different. Had he accidentally implied he had a small dick? "How do you like your steak?"

She flipped back over so she could watch the sunset once more. He wanted her to look at him again. "Slightly charred."

Josh raised a brow. "No way."

She giggled. "Yes."

"Just when I thought we were getting along."

She laughed and reached down to scratch Thor's head. "Well, let me make it worse. I was thinking about how you know all this stuff regarding Alan, and I don't even know your ex's name."

"Jeez, you really know how to keep a guy interested." He rechecked the steaks, pulled his off, and left hers to burn while shaking his head. "Natasha. I called her Tasha."

"What was she like?" Kyla asked. Josh crossed the deck to the hammock and nudged her legs. "Uh-uh. Gossip first."

He chuckled. "All right, all right. She's pretty, works at the bank, and...owns a lot of suits. I don't know." He shrugged. "Our relationship was mostly about sex."

"Well, that sounds awful." Kyla slid him a sly smile and flushed a little.

"Quite the sacrifice," he said, hoping to keep that smile on her face. Kyla sat up in the hammock, and he took the space on her left. He couldn't keep any room between them. She pressed up against his side, warm and still slightly damp from the shower. At this rate, he'd have to invest in Teflon shorts.

"And she still cheated?" Kyla shook her head. "High libido on that girl."

Josh laughed. He couldn't believe he already could. "I worked a lot."

"Not an excuse."

Josh turned to look at her. A faint dusting of freckles covered the bridge of her nose, a beauty mark sat near her left eyebrow, and she had the softest, plushest-looking lips he'd ever seen. He wanted nothing more than to take her face in his hands and kiss her, deep and slow.

The moment shattered with a trilling noise from his pocket. He stood and slid the phone out. Dylan. Silently, he passed it to Kyla. His brother wouldn't be calling him.

"Hi," she said.

Dylan's voice crackled through the speaker, but Josh couldn't make out any words. Kyla smiled briefly, and Josh's heart banged against his ribs.

Her face went pale. She furrowed her eyebrows and flattened her lips into a line.

"Yeah, maybe he's just laying low." She didn't sound convinced. Shit. That had to mean Alan couldn't be found. Kyla had a right to know about the investigation, but Josh wished, maybe selfishly, that Dylan would've solved the problem before calling. Josh didn't want her to stress.

Kyla hung up the phone and looked at him with wide, frightened eyes. He quickly sat back down on the hammock, jostling her into his side. She dropped her head onto his shoulder, and he wrapped his arms around her. God, she fit perfectly.

"I'm not gonna let anything happen to you," he murmured into her hair. "You're not alone."

"I'm scared." She sobbed. His T-shirt quickly soaked through, but he couldn't find it in him to mind. He'd do anything to make her feel better, and it seemed as if she needed a shoulder to cry on.

"I know. I'm not going anywhere." The sweet, strawberry scent of her shampoo filled his nose. He could get used to that.

"I don't want you getting hurt." Kyla clutched his waist like a life preserver in turbulent waters.

Josh had become a stranger to himself. He usually didn't like it when women cried, and Tasha always complained he never wanted to take care of her. He'd been doing his best, but he had to admit he fell short. Now, though, he wanted to be Kyla's safe harbor. He wanted to take care of her.

"I wouldn't mind getting hurt for you." The words spilled out of his mouth before he could stop them. For a moment, Kyla went still and silent. She pulled her head from his chest and stared at him. Tears still ran down her face, but her green eyes contained such awe it took Josh aback.

The world fell away. Josh realized Kyla had tipped nearly into his lap due to the angle of the hammock. She swiped away a tear on her cheek, then slowly, as though giving him time to run, she untangled her arms from his waist and wound them around his neck. God, even tearstained, she was beautiful. Her hair slipped silkily through his fingers, and the heat of her body seeped through his T-shirt.

Suddenly, her lips were on his. The kiss began soft, almost reverent. He put a hand on the side of her face and pulled her in, deepening the kiss.

He was in Dylan's college apartment, and Sky smirked as she pulled off her top.

Josh shot up from the hammock, knocking Kyla to the side.

She barely caught herself before falling. He scarcely noticed. The grill emitted thick, black smoke. Thor woke up and started barking.

Dylan had been right the whole time. Josh had the impulse control of a particularly reckless kitten. God, he didn't even know how Kyla felt about his brother.

Dylan would kill him regardless. He'd just signed his own death warrant.

Avoiding any and all eye contact, Josh licked his lips as he pulled Kyla's more than slightly charred steak off the heat.

CHAPTER ELEVEN

Dinner passed in awkward silence. Neither brought up the elephant in the room—that incredible, heart-stopping kiss. Or, what had to seem to Kyla to be Josh's instant repulsion. He pissed around on his phone while she ate her blackened steak. He didn't know how, but she seemed to enjoy the meal. That, or she wanted to be polite.

Josh wanted to ask if she liked it. Find out what else she liked, learn her little quirks, and watch her pretty eyes light up when he teased her. More than that, he wanted to forget the steak and carry her up the stairs to his bedroom. He had never been this attracted to someone. Despite only meeting only yesterday, she didn't hide anything from him. Or at least he didn't think she did. Her heart led her, and he might have ruined his chances for it to lead to him.

Fuck.

At least he'd made the problem of keeping his distance from her really simple. She'd probably never look at him again, and he could get over this ridiculous crush without hurting anyone else.

Kyla offered to wash dishes, and like a damn coward, he

accepted. He couldn't stand the silence. He wanted nothing more than to apologize for breaking off the kiss, but when Josh remembered the look of absolute betrayal on Dylan's face when he caught Josh with Sky, he fled to his room.

He took the stairs two at a time and tried not to slam his door. Dylan had put Kyla off-limits, and Josh couldn't make the same mistake of sleeping with someone Dylan had laid claim to. He punched his pillow, then threw it across the guest room. Attraction couldn't be controlled, though. It didn't follow rules or heed warnings.

Josh sat back against his headboard and grabbed his phone. He scrolled through the photos he had snapped of Kyla. In his favorite, she sat in the lawn chair at the lake, tipping back a bottle of beer for a drink while trying to hold in laughter. Her eyes had darted toward him just as he snapped the photo.

He could drown in Kyla's attention. She made him feel something he might have called contentment. He thumbed over to the next photo. Kyla carried Thor like a baby, all his paws in the air, her lips pursed to kiss him on the end of his nose.

Josh must be cursed. He and his brother had always had the same taste in women. They liked the same Spice Girl. The same sister from the house around the corner. Sky in college...

When he found Natasha in bed with another man, he'd thought of Dylan. Josh had done that to his own brother. Seeing your girlfriend fucking another man was like a gut punch, but being that other man? He couldn't believe Dylan still answered his text messages.

However, if Dylan wanted Kyla, he should have made his move on her years ago. To keep Josh away from her and play on the guilt Dylan knew Josh still carried over Sky seemed cruel.

Josh threw another pillow.

He wanted to tell Kyla the truth, but he wouldn't be the one to out Dylan's feelings for her. Dylan had to do that himself.

Kyla's footsteps sounded on the stairs. She had come up to the cabin scared and alone. He wanted to be there for her, be someone she could trust.

He hoped like hell he hadn't broken that trust by breaking the kiss.

* * *

JOSH TOSSED AND TURNED ALL NIGHT, BUT HE HAD FINALLY DEVISED A plan to fix everything. Cinnamon buns wouldn't cut it this time. He didn't want a replay of that awkward dinner at the breakfast table.

While he showered, he reviewed the plan one more time. Josh would take her out of the cabin for a change of scenery. When he felt shitty, hiking always helped. Surrounded by sky-high mountains and towering pines, he seemed small, his problems insignificant. A hike would be the perfect friendly gesture.

He dressed and grabbed the last granola bar for breakfast. He owed her a good day, and all great hikes started with trail mix.

Thor barked behind him. He jumped and clutched his chest, then turned and laughed. "Hey, buddy. Don't wake your mama, okay?" He reached down to scratch the dog behind the ears. "I'm not ready to face her yet."

Thor licked his face. God, dogs had it easy. Kiss whoever the hell you want, with no consequences. Josh grabbed his keys, and they headed to the Jeep.

West Glacier Mercantile had been around forever. Willy sold everything from tackle to hiking gear to high-end sports drinks. Josh knew him as a marketing genius and a hell of a nice guy.

His daughter, Lulu, wasn't half bad, either. She had been his first kiss the summer he turned twelve. Spin-the-bottle had been Dylan's idea. He liked the girl in the cabin down the road from them, Tiffany. Everyone liked her. The summer before, she had been one of the boys. That summer, she'd been different in a way all the boys had noticed.

Lulu, always hidden behind the counter at the store, had an understated beauty missed by most. After that kiss, though, Josh noticed her a lot.

The bells jingled over his head as he opened the wood-framed screen door. "Why, Mr. Hamilton. It's been too long."

He smiled at her singsong voice. "I agree, Lu." He held Thor's leash tightly as he picked his way through the aisles and up to the counter. Her round face had stayed pretty, but her stomach had become just as round. "When did this happen?"

She laughed and rubbed her pregnant belly. "About eight months ago in the storage room."

Josh blushed at the thought, and she winked at him. "Do I need to teach Billy a thing or two about romance?" he asked.

"Ha. He does all right in that department." Her diamond engagement ring flashed in the morning sunlight as Lu reached over the counter to pat his cheek. "How are you, Joshy? You look rough."

He grimaced. "I feel it. There's been a lot going on."

"I wish you could find someone to settle down with, Josh. You'd make a great dad one day."

He laughed off the suggestion, a dream he didn't see coming true for him anytime soon. "I'm a long way from that, Lu. I can't seem to keep a woman around me long enough to get that far."

She quirked a brow as if she didn't believe him. He wished. "Well, you have a dog, at least."

He looked down at Thor. "Dylan's. Failed police dog turned biggest baby in Montana."

"How is Dylan?"

Josh bit back a heavy sigh. "He's Dylan."

She laughed. "Tell him I miss his face."

"I'll do that." If his brother ever talked to him after that kiss with Kyla.

Lulu set a hand on her lower back. "What brings you in today?"

He sighed. "Two things. First, I need trail mix."

"You two boys hiking?"

"I'm also hoping to take a girl."

Lulu's face lit up. "You left me hanging way too damn long, Hamilton. Tell me everything."

"There's not really much to tell yet. But she's a photographer and—"

Lu pointed at him. "Baring Falls."

Josh chuckled. "I was thinking about Baring Falls. It's special, but Virginia Falls is gorgeous, too."

"Well, you know I always enjoyed our summers up at Baring Falls when we were kids. Lots of good memories up there. You were happy then."

He coughed out a laugh. "Yeah."

A lot had been different back then. He still had his mom, for one. And he and his brother had been thick as thieves. A group of them, Josh, Dylan, Lulu, Tiff, Chad, and Jer, had seen their first bear up there.

The moment had been magic with all six teenagers falling quiet to take in the natural world at its finest. The black bear had eaten some berries, turned, and left. They'd been barely twenty feet away. After that, they'd bonded. They all knew the encounter could have ended differently. Baring Falls became their place.

He wanted to share that magic with Kyla.

Lulu had just set a big bag of the deluxe trail mix, his favorite, on the counter when the door chimed.

Josh turned to see Tiffany. She laughed and ran over to pull him into a hug. "Hey, handsome." Thor barked and started wagging his tail. She reached down to pet his head. "You're handsome, too, huh?"

Josh laughed and kissed her cheek. "How are you doing?" he asked. "It's been a while."

"A year, at least. You work too hard."

He shook his head. He heard that way too damn much. It might even have been true. "How's Jer?"

"He's in the van with Chad. I just came in for tampons."

Josh laughed, pulled a twenty from his wallet, set it on the counter, and grabbed his trail mix. "On that note, I'll see you all later."

"Good to see you again, Josh," Lulu said. "Let me grab your change."

"Keep it. Or use it to cover Tiff's..."

"Tampons." She punched his shoulder. "It's like you're still a teenager."

"Bye, girls." He headed back to the parking lot. He might still be able to get back before Kyla woke up. He didn't want her to worry.

"Hamilton," a voice called. Josh stopped and tried not to wince. Jer and Chad clambered out of a sticker-coated van and came over to shake his hand. "Going hiking?"

"Hoping to." Josh didn't want to tell the guys where he planned to take Kyla. His friendly gesture had taken on a different cast in the light of Lu's teasing. He didn't want to share.

"Hey, bud," Chad said to Thor, crouching down to scratch his neck.

"We need to catch up," Josh said. "But I have a guest at the cabin, and I need to get back."

"A guest." Jer smirked. "What's her name?"

"Tasha, wasn't it?" Chad asked.

Josh had forgotten he'd told Chad about Tasha in an impromptu phone call and regretted mentioning her. He opened the Jeep door, set the trail mix inside, and lifted Thor onto the seat. "We broke up."

Jer started laughing. "You can't escape that easily."

"We'll get the truth out of you, Josh," Chad said just before Josh shut his door. He chuckled along with them and hoped they never met Kyla so he wouldn't have to clarify their relationship. He knew exactly how Chad would look at him, and Josh could do without the smirk.

Josh started the Jeep and pulled out of the small gravel lot. Kyla didn't need any more men crowding her. She already had both Hamilton brothers falling all over themselves while she ran from her ex.

Josh looked over at the dog, tongue lolling from the side of his mouth. "You think she'll come with us to the waterfall?"

Thor tilted his head and thumped his tail against the seat.

CHAPTER TWELVE

Sleep came in fits and starts. Her heart wanted to relive the heat of Josh's lips on hers, but her head kept replaying his hasty escape from the hammock.

Maybe he just didn't know what to do with a crying woman. Maybe he got caught up in the moment but regretted sending her the wrong message. Maybe she had gotten in over her head again. She wished he would just tell her instead of leaving her to guess.

Kyla padded down the stairs to find Josh and Thor gone. Again. This time, no baking, and worse, no handwritten note.

Her heart sank, though she didn't know why. There was nothing between Josh and her but friendship.

After she brewed a pot of coffee and poured herself a cup, Kyla took her mug and laptop out to the front porch to read emails and finally send a teaser to her bride and groom.

The sun had already risen, and the warm, morning light peeked at her through the pines that lined the drive. This beautiful example of light and shadow would be perfect for the students who had signed up for her photography workshop.

She set her cup down, then ran inside to grab her camera.

Back on the porch, Kyla snapped a couple of shots and immediately uploaded them to her computer. She had captured one particularly pretty picture that featured the water glinting through the trees—the foreground dotted with white wildflowers. She posted the image to her photography blog. Hopefully, that would help fill the last three vacant workshop slots.

She pulled up her email, meaning to send Matt and Sharon her favorite shot of them dancing under strings of fairy lights, but got distracted by a late-night email from Dylan.

Rosy,

Still no luck tracking Alan. Checked with his secretary and the new girlfriend. Yes, there's a new one. I'm thinking of heading up to the cabin. I hate to leave you alone in the woods without knowing Alan's whereabouts.

She nodded slowly, testing her emotional state. After Josh's rejection, she would have expected a new sexual conquest of Alan's to send her spiraling, but she could only think that someone new would take too much of his time for him to follow her to Glacier.

She took a long swallow of coffee and closed her eyes to savor the almost chocolatey flavor. Maybe she hadn't seen Alan's sports car in the driveway, after all. Clearly, her judgment had taken a hit this week.

After another sip, she shot Dylan a quick response.

No, don't miss work for me. I need you home to figure this out. We'll do a weekend in Vegas after wedding season if you want a vacation.

Kyla hit send, then shook out her hands. The tension in her shoulders hadn't lessened since Josh leaped out of the hammock.

In truth, she didn't want to see anyone else until she and Josh talked. Kyla had gone out on a limb, certain she'd read the signs correctly, but Josh had pretty much run screaming from her lips.

Two rejections, Josh and Alan, back-to-back. How much could a girl take?

Despite last night's disaster, she enjoyed Josh's company. His cooking. His wit. His sexy body, those lips... Ugh. No. The lips were off-limits.

She wanted to take things further with him because she hadn't been this attracted to a man in years. If only she'd picked a man who felt attracted to her.

Kyla groaned.

Gravel crunched, and her heart skipped a beat. Alan? Dylan? She leaped up, peering down the driveway. Josh's Jeep rolled to a stop, and she closed her laptop on a sigh.

She had no idea how today would pan out, no way of gauging Josh's mood, but her stomach still blossomed with butterflies as he stepped out of the car.

Josh offered her a wave and a duck of the head, then moved around the front of the vehicle to lift Thor from the passenger side. The puppy ran up the deck, tail wagging, and jumped on her legs in greeting.

"Hi, baby. Where were you?" She looked up at Josh as he mounted the deck, and her breath caught in her throat. He wore a tight, gray T-shirt and cargo shorts, essentially his uniform at the cabin so far, but he looked even better than he had the night before. His skin looked sun-kissed, with a faint sheen of sweat along his hairline. He avoided her gaze, though.

"Sorry I didn't leave a note." He rubbed the back of his neck. "Just ran to the store for some trail mix."

"Trail mix, huh? Are we hiking?" Maybe if she avoided mentioning the kiss altogether, they could get back to being friends.

He laughed. "You figured me out. I'm going up to grab my gear. You ready to get out of the house, or do you have work to do?"

"I'm ready to see more of our beautiful state. I just need to put my hiking boots on." Josh lowered his gaze to her bare feet, and she noticed a smile playing on his lips before he opened the front door and headed inside.

Kyla lingered on the porch swing and cuddled the overgrown puppy. "You're going to have to keep me in check today," she whispered in his ear. "Your uncle is a dreamboat, but I can't take any more rejection."

Thor licked her face, and she laughed before getting up to follow Josh inside.

"What were you two talking about?" Josh asked.

"Nothing." She hoped he didn't notice the heat rising on her face as she brushed past him to climb the stairs.

* * *

When they stepped into the midday heat of a humid Montana summer, Josh held his arms out and tipped his head back to face the sun. "God, I love summertime in the mountains."

She laughed when Thor jumped at Josh and barked.

Josh leaned down to scruff his fur just as Kyla reached for his collar to clip on his leash. Hummingbirds danced in her chest when their fingers brushed. Just as quickly, his hand slipped away from hers with Thor's leash.

"I'll walk him so you can enjoy the scenery. I've seen it all a hundred times."

"I'll bet it's still just as pretty the hundredth time." A light breeze caressed her overheated skin, but Kyla managed to keep her smile as she composed herself again. Josh did not reciprocate her feelings. She knew that now. He had only just ended his relationship a couple of days before. She'd had six weeks to get over the same thing, and she still struggled with residual feelings of betrayal.

They strolled up the dirt road toward a trailhead, Thor leading the way. Despite the awkwardness on the hammock, Josh had a comfortable presence—like Dylan, but quieter. No less confident, just less loud. Josh had a mysterious side, which she found incredibly sexy.

"So, where are you taking me?" That seemed like a safe enough question, and she couldn't take the silence much longer.

"Baring Falls. In my opinion, one of the prettiest places in the state." He shrugged. "I thought you might want to take a couple of shots. Satisfy that photographer's itch."

Kyla smiled. "Photographer's itch, huh? Care to tell me what that is?"

"I'm assuming it's like when I get in the kitchen, and I'm dying to bake something, bring life to a new recipe, take basic ingredients, and turn them into something delicious. So, for you, that itch would be a desire to capture beauty in ways only you can see, maybe." Josh paused for a moment, his eyes reflecting an inner self-consciousness. "I would actually love to see this place through your eyes."

Josh didn't need to be self-consciousness. His words, his thoughts, were all beautiful. She just didn't know what to do with them anymore. Kyla stared off the edge of the path.

"You okay?" he asked.

"I'm—"

Josh's phone rang in his pocket, and after a glance at the screen, his mouth thinned. He turned off the phone and shoved it back.

"Dylan?"

"I wish," he said. He gently pulled Thor's leash to make him heel as a young couple passed them on the trail, hand-in-hand. They looked so carefree, so happy. Why couldn't she have that?

Their route led them up an inclined path, and Kyla brushed sweat from her forehead.

"Now, what were we talking about?" he asked.

Kyla stopped, and Josh turned to face her. She wanted nothing more than to reach up and cradle his handsome face, stand on her toes, and press her lips to his. She wanted him to catch her bottom lip between his and suck gently. She wanted to laugh with him while she pulled back to steady her quickened heartbeat and weakened knees.

Despite her wants, she didn't. Kyla knew she had flaws, but at least she never made the same mistake twice.

"Something about how you were going to bake us something incredible in your amazing kitchen later tonight," she said.

The stress seemed to release from his shoulders, and he gave her an easy smile. "Is that what I said, huh?"

"Mm. That's exactly what you said." She pulled a bottle of water from her backpack and crouched down. "Thor, sweetie. Come get a drink." She cupped her hand, poured some water in, and the puppy lapped it up.

"You're a good dog mom."

"Thank you. I never receive enough compliments." She laughed.

"I find that hard to believe." Josh raised an eyebrow. "You seem like a great girl."

"Well, Dylan said I have a nice ass." *Goddammit. Stop, Kyla. Josh doesn't want you like that.*

Josh frowned. "Well, he's right. Kind of odd for a best friend to say, though. Does he say things like that a lot?"

Kyla shrugged, then stood and wiped her wet hands on the seat of her shorts. "I can go ahead if you need to return that call."

"Nah." He shook his head. "I have nothing to say to my ex."

Kyla nodded slowly. "I understand."

"I don't want her to get in the way of this incredible hike." Josh looked around. Kyla followed his gaze over the gorgeous ferns, saplings, and new life among the deep shadows of the forest. "I don't want her back. I need to move on."

CHAPTER THIRTEEN

Kyla held her camera to her eye and framed Josh front and center, the waterfall cascading behind him. Sunglasses covered his eyes, but his pouty lips and scruffy chin were on full display. He rested his hands casually on his narrow hips, and the sleeves of his T-shirt stretched tight around his biceps. The man looked hot.

Thank god photography gave her an excuse to stare.

"Okay. One more." Kyla could truly do this all day, but they'd been shooting for twenty minutes already. Worse, she couldn't even use any of the ones with Josh for her workshop. She just couldn't resist a gorgeous man against a gorgeous backdrop.

"Cheese." Josh made a goofy face as he posed for yet another photo. He hadn't complained once, and the thought made her heart go pitter-patter in a terribly unhelpful way.

"That's a great one." She lowered her camera to watch him watching her.

She must have taken at least fifty shots of the waterfall before she turned her focus on him and took fifty more. She had even captured some great photos of Thor in the water. He romped around in the stream and jumped to catch bumblebees from the air, thankfully missing every time. The dog made a natural model. She planned to frame her favorite shot for Dylan's birthday next month.

"Done?" Josh asked, hands out to his sides, showcasing the falls.

She snapped one more. "Mm. Yes." She lowered her camera and tucked an escaped strand of hair from her ponytail behind her ear. "Thank you."

"Not a problem." He smiled easily before he sauntered to the edge of the stream, slid his sunglasses off his face, and tucked them in the V-neck of his T-shirt. He leaned down and tossed a stick for Thor. Kyla lifted her camera one last time. She adjusted the lens to focus on his blue eyes, then snapped several frames as Josh sat down on the edge of the stream and untied his boots.

"What are you doing?" she asked.

He looked up at her, mischief in his eyes.

"Getting my feet wet. Want to join Thor and me?"

She rarely took chances or risks, and especially not dares.

"Isn't it cold?"

"Freezing," he said with emphasis. A small smile crept across his face.

"Oh, what the hell."

She packed her camera in her backpack, took off her shoes and socks, and stepped slowly into the water. Kyla winced. Josh hadn't been understating things. Thor bounded toward her, splashing the icy water up her bare thighs. She squealed, and he barked.

A few feet deeper in, Josh observed her with a wide grin.

She took a few more tentative steps into the water. "You weren't kidding about the cold." She shivered and wheeled her arms as she almost slipped on the slick stones under her feet.

"Whoa, easy." Josh waded over and grasped her hand to steady her. She repressed another shiver. Not from the cold but from the heat of his palm on hers and the carefree smile on his face. "Refreshing, though, right?"

"I guess you could call it that."

"But you're having fun? I'd hate to get a bad review." He let go of her hand and winked before bending to splash some water for Thor to chase.

"You get five stars." Despite the awkwardness of last night and the chill on her legs, she'd never had a better time in the woods. "And you're a great dog uncle."

He laughed. "High praise. Dylan and I had a dog when we were kids. An overweight basset hound named Nigel."

"He sounds adorable."

"He was great. Nowhere near the energy of this guy."

"Thor is the best. I've been puppysitting while Dylan is at work most days, so, technically, he's half-mine."

Josh snorted. "Bet you've never said that to Dylan's face."

Kyla laughed. "Nope."

"He's kind of possessive." Josh's eyebrows furrowed. He watched Thor, but his thoughts had clearly wandered elsewhere.

"I think he would prefer *protective*," Kyla said.

Josh shook his head, then cleared his throat. "You're protective of him, too, huh? You're really close?"

Josh's question seemed to suggest he was fishing for information about Kyla's and Dylan's dynamic, as if he wanted to ascertain their relationship. Did that mean Josh was interested in her but thought she was interested in Dylan? Her heart gave a little flip. "He's a great guy, a great friend, and has really been there for me since the breakup."

"So—" Josh said.

"Hey, bro," someone called from the path.

Two men and a woman, all about Kyla's age, dressed for a long hike and wearing large packs and with bear spray canisters clipped to their belts, lumbered toward the water's edge. Thor took off running in their direction and jumped up on the one guy, who pulled his shirt off as they approached.

The man took the puppy in stride and rubbed Thor's ears. "Hey, buddy."

"Sorry," Kyla called out. "I should have him on the leash."

"Don't worry about it." The guy smiled in her direction.

"Chad, buddy. I didn't know you guys were coming up here." Josh strode back to the shore. Thor trotted over to him and sat down for a neck scratch. "Hey, Jer. Tiff."

Kyla stared at Josh's back. He clearly knew these people, but his shoulders were tense. If she didn't know any better, she'd say he's put himself between the other hikers and her.

"Seeing you this morning reminded us how great these falls are," Chad said. This morning? How much had Kyla missed? "Come over later for a few beers. We're having a fire. Your new lady is also welcome."

Josh looked at her, his expression unreadable. "What do you say?"

Unable to determine what Josh wanted her to say, she shrugged.

Josh turned back to Chad. "I'll call you later. Let you know." Josh shook Chad's hand. Josh hadn't disagreed with his buddy's assumption that Josh and Kyla were together. Interesting.

Josh's friends headed back to the trailhead, and Thor trailed after his new hike mates. She whistled for him to return, and he trotted back.

Josh took hold of Thor's collar and reattached the leash. She stared at his ass as he leaned over. Quite the view. Distracted, she'd forgotten to keep an eye on the fickle Montana skies.

Light raindrops began to fall, and Kyla's breath caught in

her throat. She had left her backpack open and her camera exposed. She raced back to the shoreline, but her toe caught a rock. Kyla cried out, threw her arms out for balance, and landed on her knees in the icy water. Thor pounced to her side, soaking her shirt and licking her face. Frigid cold enveloped her.

"Kyla!" Josh instantly reached her side and swung her up into his arms. He took three long strides out of the water and set her on the shore, then crouched in front of her as Thor parked beside them and panted. Josh's warm hands brought gooseflesh to her cold calves.

"Are you hurt?" He moved his hands over her wrists, checking for breaks and cuts, she assumed.

"More embarrassed than hurt." Raindrops landed on her cheeks, and she remembered her camera. She reached over, zipped up her bag, then grabbed her socks and shoes. "Thank you for the rescue."

He winked. "You're in luck. My rescue services are free today."

She rubbed her arms to ward off the chill, which was ineffectual, then gingerly slipped a sock over the toe she stubbed. "What else do these services include?"

His brows shot up in surprise, but he smiled. She carefully donned the rest of her footwear.

"How about a free shuttle service to the bottom of the trail?" he asked.

The rain picked up, further soaking her clothes. She hadn't expected anything intensive when she got up in the morning, so she'd thrown on a thin white T-shirt and a black and navy lace bra to go with her hiking shorts. Unfortunately, between the rain and the river, her shirt had turned nearly see-through and clung to her every curve. Worse, the thin lace of the cups did nothing to hide her hardened nipples. She wanted to blame that on the cold, but as Josh's gaze flickered down and back up, they tightened further.

She had to get to the cabin as quickly as possible.

Kyla thought about her toe and grimaced. "Shuttle, huh?"

"Why not? I'm sure you're as light as a feather."

He grabbed Thor's leash and knotted it to his belt loop, then slung Kyla's backpack over his shoulder and, without much effort, lifted her in his arms. She shivered at the warmth of his arms against her cold body. He clutched her close and began the trek down the mountain, Thor trotting beside them.

The rain fell harder as Josh broke into a jog. Kyla wrapped her arms around his neck and held tight. Being this close to his body, she couldn't help but let her mind stray back to yesterday, to the hammock, their thighs pressed against each other, and their lips locked in a kiss she would never forget.

CHAPTER FOURTEEN

The rain had utterly soaked Kyla and Josh by the time the two of them reached the cabin steps. The smell of petrichor rose in the air, and thunder roared beyond the mountains. The full-on thunderstorm hadn't reached them, but the clouds blocked the sun and turned the afternoon into twilight, making it feel as if they were the only two people in the world. The day had become romantic in a way she couldn't allow.

"We made it." Josh breathed against her cheek. For a wild moment she thought he would kiss her, but Thor barked his excitement, obviously having enjoyed the run in the rain as much as she had.

Josh shifted her in his arms and dug in his front pocket for his keys. Thor tugged at the lead, nearly pulling them over, so Josh untied the leash from his belt.

"You can set me down," she said, amused at his dedication to her barely sore toe.

Not only had Josh carried her all the way home for nothing but a bruised ego, he had told her silly jokes as he jogged through the summer shower—something about priests in bars and men from Nantucket.

"Knights in shining armor don't do things like that."

She quirked a brow. "Oh, no?"

"No, ma'am. They finish the job. There." He inserted the key, and the lock clicked. Josh bumped the door open with his hip, then stepped inside. Thor pushed past them and shook, spattering them both again.

"Doesn't look like the rain will let up anytime soon." Josh kicked the door closed behind them, then crossed to the couch and set Kyla down. She immediately started soaking through the throw pillows, but he didn't seem to notice.

Thor bounded over and parked his butt on the floor next to Josh.

"Looks like we're stuck in here, huh?" she asked.

Josh's eyes were alight with an emotion she couldn't quite place. "So it seems." He ran his palm over one of her knees, then the other. "You sure you're all right? Don't need any of my excellent first aid skills?"

"I'm fine. Thanks for the lift back."

Kyla didn't make the same mistake twice. She would ignore the ambiance, the closeness, and the fact he could see right through her shirt to the lingerie underneath. She glanced at Thor, who shook one more time.

Josh shrugged as if carrying her hundred and twenty pounds down a mountain had been no big deal. "I feel bad. I dragged you into the water with me."

"I'm a big girl. I make my own choices."

Josh grinned. "Then you fell."

Kyla shoved his shoulder. He captured her hand in his and brought it to his lips. His gaze didn't leave hers as he pressed his warm mouth against the back of her hand. Fire shone in those deep, blue eyes. She almost forgot she'd gotten frozen and drenched. She almost forgot the humiliation in the hammock.

"I want to make you feel better, Kyla." The low timbre of his voice melted her.

She sucked in a deep breath. She hadn't expected him to switch from funny to fuckable in the blink of an eye. "Honestly, you're doing a pretty good job so far."

A back-of-the-hand kiss didn't mean anything. Hell, Dylan had kissed the back of her hand when she smashed it against his countertop last month. The look in Josh's eyes, though...

He pressed one slow kiss after another to her hand, her fingertips, and the inside of her wrist. "I think I can do better. In fact—" He slid his lips up her arm and looked as if he was about to lick the rainwater off her skin when his phone rang.

"Fuck." He gave her a sheepish grin, then dug his phone from his pocket and glanced at the screen. His smile vanished. "Let me go grab you a towel."

He jumped to his feet, then headed past the kitchen and down the short hall.

"What was that about?" She ran her hands over Thor's wet fur, half petting him, half holding him off the furniture. His tail thumped against the coffee table, and she smiled.

She looked down at her wrist where Josh had kissed her. Her skin still tingled where hips lips had touched her. His kisses hadn't felt like friendly kisses.

However, she couldn't forget the preceding night, the panic on his face, and the distance he'd kept until she'd fallen. Josh had been clear that kissing her ranked pretty low on his vacation to-do list. Kyla would not let herself get suckered again, no matter how gorgeous Josh Hamilton was or how warmly he kissed. Perhaps his phone ringing had been for the best.

Josh emerged, two towels in hand, and crossed the room to her. "Your towel, milady."

He tossed her a fluffy white towel, then scooped Thor up

and wrapped him in the other. Josh laughed as Thor bit the end and tugged.

"I love him." Kyla squeezed the moisture from her hair.

"Yeah, he's a great dog." Josh set him down, and he immediately raced upstairs. "In fact, he's lucky he's cute enough to get away with his behavior."

His phone rang again. Josh canceled the call, then tossed the silent phone onto the other end of the couch.

"What if it's important?" Kyla asked.

He looked at her. "It's not. I promise."

Kyla nodded and bit her lip. She should change, then maybe they could watch another movie.

"So." He sat down beside her, so close his shoulder brushed hers. Josh made it hard to want to be anywhere else. "I should apologize about before."

"Before?"

"You're going to make me say it, huh?" He offered her a tight smile.

She looked at him, and his blue eyes seemed to swallow her. He leaned against her, warm and wet from the rain. The heat rippled through the rest of her body.

"I'm sorry about kissing you," he said. Her heart dropped. Right. "I mean, I'm not. You're goddamn gorgeous and..."

"You think I'm gorgeous?" Kyla started to feel like she'd go crazy if he mixed one more signal. What did this guy want from her?

He smirked. "You're gorgeous and know it." His gaze moved over her face and seemed to linger on her lips.

"Is this about your girlfriend?" She hazily remembered the gin-soaked nights after Alan, a fog of weeping and crappy TV.

Josh shrugged. "She cheated on me. It sucks, but that's life." He took her hand in his. "Forget about her. I'm trying to say something. I like you. I think you're great. I think you're sexy as hell."

"But?" Kyla could feel the 'but' coming a mile away. At least she'd have an explanation for his ridiculous behavior.

"But..." Josh huffed out a sigh. Then, he pulled her hand back up his mouth and kissed the inside of her wrist once more. "But nothing. I want to kiss you. I think you want me to."

Kyla's breath caught. She searched his eyes and found nothing but honesty. Josh wanted to kiss her. She slid her fingers into his hair and caressed his cheek with her thumb. He pressed a kiss to the palm of her hand. Then, he turned to kiss her lips. She wanted nothing more than to climb on top of him, to get close and never pull away. Instead, she braced for him to run.

Josh smiled. "Stop thinking."

She huffed. "Can't help it."

"Just enjoy it." He leaned his head into her hand. The barest scrape of stubble lit her nerve endings on fire. "We could just have tonight. No strings, no complications. Forget ex-girl-friends and ex-fiancés. Forget break-ins and stubbed toes. Forget everything outside this cabin, this room, this moment." He looked up at her, and she realized he felt vulnerable. "Tell me to stop if you think this is a crazy idea."

She inhaled shakily. "I... I don't want you to stop."

"You sure? We could just watch *The Creature from the Black Lagoon* again."

Kyla teetered for a moment. She knew Josh meant his offer. They really could just watch a movie, no hard feelings. She ran her thumb across the plane of his cheek.

"Tempting," she said. "But..."

"Not as tempting as me?" He grinned. Slowly, she nodded. He leaned close and pressed a soft kiss to the corner of her lips.

"Just tonight." She leaned in.

His mouth covered hers, and she closed her eyes. His lips were warm and soft, but his kiss was hard and passionate. She couldn't doubt he wanted this anymore, and when he flicked the seam of her lips with his tongue, she opened for him. She wanted more. His tongue caressed hers, and Kyla shivered.

She didn't mind being his one-night stand, his rebound, his anything. She wanted this intense lust, this urge to consume and be consumed by a relative stranger—no strings, no pressure, and none of the complicated emotions that came from a relationship. She needed to stop thinking and just enjoy his hands on her body, hers on his. His taste, his touch, his kiss.

She grasped his shoulders, swung a leg over his lap, and straddled him. His wet T-shirt clung to his chest and shoulders, and she ached to touch his bare skin.

She tugged at the bottom of his shirt. Josh lifted his arms as she pulled the fabric over his head. Kyla caught sight of the words *Until we meet again...* tattooed over his heart. She traced the words with trembling fingers. A memorial for his mother?

Josh covered her hand with his, and she met his gaze. "I'm sorry," she whispered. "I shouldn't have—"

A corner of his mouth ticked upward slightly. "It's nice to share with someone who knows what happened. I don't like explaining."

"There's no need."

A heartbeat passed, then he pulled her against him and kissed her. She kissed him back, startled at the revelation of his tattoo, his heart. For a moment, the encounter stopped feeling like just a fun afternoon.

Josh yanked her closer, then flipped her over onto her back and straddled her. His wet shorts, cold against her bare legs, contrasted with the warmth of his bare chest. He winked at her gasp, then took her mouth once more.

Kyla caressed his arms with her fingertips. Josh was one

hundred percent unadulterated masculinity. Strong yet gentle, and oh, so heavenly. He trailed a finger along the side of her breast, down her abdomen, and past her waist to the curve of her hip.

"You should probably get those wet clothes off. You must be cold." His breath, warm against her throat, made her shiver.

"Yes," she said in a breathy voice she didn't quite recognize as her own.

"You sure?" he whispered.

She nodded and bit her lip. His gaze locked on her mouth, and his eyes darkened. Her pulse jumped. Josh took a deep breath that pressed the planes of his hard chest into the softer curve of her breasts. The juncture between her legs throbbed.

He lifted a brow in question.

"My shirt first."

He pressed a kiss to the tip of her nose, and her heart pounded with the anticipation of another deep kiss. Instead, he sat back on his haunches and grasped the bottom of her shirt.

"Lift your arms," he said softly.

She did, and he pulled the shirt over her head. He reached for the buttons on her shorts and popped them open. She lifted her hips, and Josh wiggled the shorts off her legs. He kissed her hip and breathed in her rain-soaked skin. She shivered again.

"Damn," he whispered as he gazed at her nearly nude body.

Kyla turned her face to the side. His gaze was too much. With a gentle touch to her chin, he encouraged her to look back at him.

"What's wrong?" he asked.

"I'm just a little nervous."

"Nervous?" He frowned. "Why? It hasn't been that long since you've been with a man, has it?"

"No, of course not. I was engaged. Remember?"

"Right. I knew that. I'm just"—he ran his palm up and

down her forearm—"getting this vibe you're inexperienced. Not that there's anything wrong with that."

Her cheeks reddened.

"Oh, god. I'm sorry. Dammit. I'm an ass. I'm not trying to insult you. You are a sexy woman, Kyla. Very sexy." He dropped his head and groaned. "I screwed this up, didn't I? I should keep my mouth shut."

She shook her head, trying not to overthink things. "You didn't screw up. But, honestly, Josh, these last few minutes have held more passion, more spontaneity than my entire sex life. So, if I'm a little skittish, it's because, honestly, this *is* all new."

Alan had been comfortable. He'd known how to take care of her and always seemed to get the job done. But if Alan had been a reliable Chevy with the features she needed, Josh was a shiny, red Maserati. He made her pulse leap in her throat, her heart hammer in her chest, and the rest of her body ache with need for him.

She could never be satisfied by "good enough" again.

He grinned and quirked a brow. "Well, if that's the case, tonight will be fun."

CHAPTER FIFTEEN

Josh froze as Kyla sat back up. Had he done something else wrong?

When she pushed him back on the sofa and straddled his thighs, he breathed a sigh of relief. She just wanted control. As long as she didn't plan on stopping this, he wouldn't complain.

His cock jerked with desire. She grasped his bare shoulders and pulled him into a sitting position. The black and blue bra keeping him from her spectacular breasts looked even sexier without a T-shirt in the way, but he cursed it at that moment.

He smiled. "You're taking the lead, huh?"

Two seconds of silence passed, then she brushed her lips against his mouth. "Yes."

He grasped her hips and pressed her against his cock. "I like that."

"Stop. You're cheating." Kyla kissed him, then giggled when he caressed her thighs with his fingertips.

"Ticklish?"

"Maybe."

He hummed. He loved learning these details about her. Josh slid his tongue across her bottom lip. He wanted to taste every inch of her rain-dampened skin. He slid a hand up to her neck, enjoying the tempting warmth. Her pulse point pounded against his hand. Did he need to slow down?

She rolled her mons against his cock. His brain whited out for a moment, and heat built into an all-too-familiar pressure in his abdomen.

"You like that?" she whispered.

"Too much, too fast. I want you, Kyla." He grasped her hips to steady himself and stop her from rubbing against him again. "I want this to last."

Kyla reached behind her back and unclasped her bra. He held his breath as she slid her bra strap down one arm, then the other. He'd been right. She had absolutely spectacular breasts.

Josh gathered her into him and kissed her.

She tasted so sweet, better than any cookie or pastry he had ever created. With his palms flat on her back, he pulled her closer, and she wrapped her arms around his neck.

Kyla skimmed her fingernails across his skin, which lit him on fire. Her forwardness surprised him. She had acted so timidly when he first met her. He liked that about her. A lot. But this side of her... Fuck. Perfect. Josh rolled so she lay beneath him yet again.

Josh unbuckled his belt, then unzipped his wet shorts and shunted them down his legs.

"In a hurry, there, Hamilton?" She smirked. He didn't miss how her gaze never drifted above his waist.

"No hurry at all." Josh stepped out of his shorts with a grin.

Kyla sat up and surprised him when she tugged at the waistband of his boxer briefs and stole a peek inside. He lifted a brow.

"What?" She looked up at him, and he got lost in her sexy green eyes. "I don't like being naked all alone."

"Your wish is my command." Josh shoved his underwear over his hips and rigid cock.

Her mouth opened in a soft O.

His cock hardened even more.

"You're not quite naked yet," he murmured.

"Oh, this old thing." She hooked her thumbs in the lacy waistband of her panties and shimmied out of them. Her boldness, coupled with her beautiful nude body, left him breathless and very, very aroused.

"Okay. That's it." He spotted Thor, who busily gnawed on a chew toy in the kitchen. He hadn't noticed the dog come back downstairs. Obviously, Josh had been preoccupied. "I'm not doing this with an audience." Not to mention, the couch didn't have nearly enough space for what he had in mind.

Josh scooped Kyla into his arms and carried her up the stairs to the master bedroom. Then he laid her on the sheets before opening the bedside table and pulling out a condom. She sat up and swiped the foil package from his hand, then tore it open with a smirk.

Josh gritted his teeth as she slowly, slowly rolled the condom onto him. Her touch, her hot little fingers, were almost too much. "That feels amazing."

She winked at him and stroked her hand over his length. "And to think we're just getting started."

"I like the sound of that." He lifted her left foot to his lips. "Is this the one that hurts?"

She nodded, and he closed his mouth over her toe.

Kyla gasped when he circled his tongue around the digit. "What are you doing?"

He released the toe from his mouth. "Hopefully turning you on?"

She nodded. "Mmm."

He licked the arch of her foot, and when he nibbled at the

sensitive skin, she gasped. He kneeled on the foot of the bed and moved his kisses over her shapely calf. "You have incredible legs."

"Thank you. Hurry up." Her hands already fisted the sheets.

Josh knew when to do what he was told. Her legs were cool under his mouth until he reached the apex of her thighs. He nipped at her inner thigh and breathed in her scent. He couldn't remember ever being this turned on.

He wrapped his arms around her hips, holding her legs open, and dove in. As he slipped his tongue between Kyla's folds, she cried out, rocked her hips against his face, and threaded a hand into his hair. He hummed against her wet slit and teased her clit with just the softest touch of his tongue.

She tasted like honey and moaned like she wanted more. He kept up the teasing. She continued to mewl, gasp, and cry out. When she let go of his hair, he looked up. She ran her hands over her body, into her hair, down her neck, and to her breasts in a frantic rhythm. That had to be the sexiest thing he'd ever seen.

Finally, he gave her what she begged for. No more teasing. He lapped at her, circled her clit, and did anything and everything he could to make her scream.

Her legs tightened around his head, her whole body shuddered, and she called out his name.

She lay panting for a moment after.

Thor barked downstairs, and Kyla lifted her head to look at Josh. She wore the sweetest smile, but her eyes were still wild. She wasn't finished, and Josh wasn't even close to done with her.

"Should we check on him?" she asked.

"Not yet."

Josh crawled on top of her, his knees between her spread

thighs, and looked down. Kyla closed her pretty eyes, and she hummed as he moved his hands to caress her hips, her sides.

Despite her smudged makeup and wet hair, she looked fucking incredible. His chest tightened.

One night only.

She opened her eyes and wrapped her long legs around his hips. He gently thrust against her mound. She whimpered, and he forced back the compulsion to drive into her. He brushed her mouth with his, and she lifted her head to deepen the kiss.

"Josh, please." His name on her lips sent a shock through him.

He fitted his cock to her opening and eased inside. Her inner walls tightened around him, and he gritted his teeth against the need to yank back. With great care, he drew back, then thrust forward. In response, Kyla tightened her grip on his shoulders.

He groaned when she pulled his face down to hers and kissed him, then thought he would lose his mind when she sucked on his tongue in time with his next thrust.

She lifted her hips to meet his movements. He drove deep and hard. She gasped. "Holy shit."

"Are you coming again?" he asked, digging his fingers into her hips.

"Yes." She swallowed. "But please, don't stop."

He had stamina in spades, but not enough to make one night last forever.

CHAPTER SIXTEEN

Birds sang outside the window of the master bedroom. The rain had stopped, and there looked to be some late-day sunlight fighting its way through the clouds.

She shivered at the memory of Josh's warm hands on her naked body and his lips tasting and nipping at her skin. She had never felt so desirable, so sensuous as when he made love to her. They'd shared more than just sex. When he hadn't been between her legs making her see stars, he had stared into her eyes.

They'd connected.

Josh took his time as if they had forever to discover each other's bodies. After the first glorious time she'd had him inside her, and even after her first, second, and third orgasm, he hadn't stopped.

His fingers were magic. He'd caressed her lips and traced the dips and curves of her body—and his mouth... God, his mouth was just as tantalizing. He had licked, sucked, and tasted every square inch of her body, leaving her a quivering but sated woman. She had never experienced pure, unadulterated bliss as she had in Josh's arms.

Before Josh, Alan had been her only lover. She'd always wanted to get to know a man first, though the thought made her laugh now. Their first time had been clumsy. The rest had been mechanical. She'd never considered Alan a selfish lover until she'd experienced what Josh had to offer. He had been gentle while he consumed her.

Kyla rolled over to look at the man who had given her hours of endless pleasure. Instead, she found Thor staring at her, tongue lolling and tail wagging. He whimpered and greeted her with a sloppy kiss.

"Hi, baby. Don't wake your Uncle Josh." He dropped his nose on the pillow, and Kyla stroked his fur. Her heart fluttered. Josh must have let Thor in bed with them after she fell asleep. Totally perfect. Too bad Josh didn't want more because, god, did she want him again.

Kyla propped up on one arm to look at him. His chest remained gloriously bare, with only a light dusting of hair over his pecs and a thin cotton sheet covering his hips. By the telltale bulge, she could tell his dreams were very, very pleasant, and she didn't have the heart to wake him. Not just yet. He looked so peaceful.

Kyla eased out of bed, then slipped on her new pink lace bra and panty set and her satin robe. She had no reason to be shy. Not after she had given her body to him completely.

After one last glance at Josh, she tiptoed down the stairs with Thor on her heels and hooked him to his leash. "Come on, cutie."

The air was cool on her skin, so she wished she'd put on pants, but she hadn't noticed anyone in the neighboring cabins, so she didn't need them for modesty. However, after Thor did his business, she ran back inside, just in case.

Kyla fed Thor, then decided to make some pancakes and bacon for dinner because they were her favorite, and she was famished. Maybe after she and Josh had something to eat, they could talk.

They could even be friends. She could be mature enough to accept that—on the outside, maybe, but her heart wanted Josh Hamilton for far more than friendship. She'd just met this man but didn't want to let him go and prayed he didn't mean it when he said tonight only, no strings.

Then there was Dylan. Even if there could be more between Josh and her, she fretted about her best friend. He might not like that she'd slept with his brother, and she worried if she should tell him and what he would say.

Kyla shook her head. Worries tomorrow. She turned on a top-forties station and began to dance a little. She couldn't remember the last time she'd been this happy. Alan felt like a distant memory.

She started the bacon frying, then rummaged through the cupboards for a large mixing bowl and a whisk. In about ten minutes, Josh would be eating the best pancakes in the state, or so Andrea had always told her.

Kyla grabbed another skillet from the cupboard above the stove and added a big dollop of butter.

Thump.

Kyla turned to look over her shoulder. Green leaves waved placidly outside the window next to the door. That sounded like it came from outside.

Bang.

This time, she knew it had.

Thor ran to the door and whined, his tail wagging. He never would have made it in the K9 unit. Needing to get a better look outside, Kyla took a deep breath, then stepped toward the door. The doorknob rattled.

Kyla hurried back to the kitchen to shut off the gas, then

tightened her robe, grabbed the biggest, pointiest knife from the butcher block, and headed for the window.

She didn't know what she expected to see on the other side of the door. Freddie Krueger? Alan? Regardless, she never would have guessed an honest-to-god blonde bombshell. Big hair, big breasts, big smile loaded with sparkling bleached teeth. She even wore one of those cute pant suits women in high-power positions from big cities on the East Coast with window-walled corner offices wear.

Kyla swung the door open out of surprise more than anything else.

"Oh, hello." The Marilyn Monroe lookalike's smile faltered, but only for a second. She looked just as confused by Kyla's presence. That, or the knife in Kyla's hand had caught her off guard. Well, at least they were even.

Thor pounced on the woman, bouncing and jumping against her legs. She pushed at him, trying to keep him off.

"Oh, sorry about him." Kyla set her weapon on the book-shelf by the door, then pulled Thor off by his collar. The all-too-short hem of her robe rose, and she yanked it down. Why hadn't she put on pants? "Can I help you?" Thor sat beside her but whined. She imagined he wanted the woman gone as much as Kyla did.

The Marilyn wannabe hadn't introduced herself, but in truth, Kyla knew exactly who she was.

Natasha.

The woman's confident smile made Kyla shrink. "This is Josh Hamilton's cabin, isn't it?"

"Yeah."

The woman laughed as she stepped inside. Kyla had never heard a more fake laugh in her life, but the crystalline tinkle still charmed her. She stepped back, and Natasha took in the cabin with pursed lips.

"Well," she said, apparently done with the niceties. "I'm here to meet my boyfriend, Josh. He's here." She didn't ask this time. "I passed his Jeep at the end of the driveway."

This woman looked like Kyla's opposite in every way that counted: tall, slim, and businesslike. Worse, according to her, she was still in a relationship with the man Kyla had just made love to. The man she was making dinner for. The man who had gotten nonstop phone calls the entire time she'd known him.

Her stomach sank. On the phone, Dylan had said, "girl trouble." Josh was the first person to say he had just become single. He'd also suggested one night, no strings.

Natasha seemed so confident. So had Josh.

"So. Josh. Where is he?"

"Um…" Kyla took another step back. She couldn't say in bed, not in the middle of the afternoon. Natasha swept her gaze languidly over Kyla's attire, and a tiny smirk spread across her face. Kyla wanted to curl up into a little ball.

"I'm Natasha Renault." She pronounced her last name with what sounded like a beautiful French-Canadian accent.

"Oh, um. I'm Kyla." God, it had gotten warm in here. How had she gotten so warm without any clothes on?

"He hasn't mentioned you." Tasha crinkled her nose slightly. Kyla felt her face ignite as Tasha's gaze lingered on Kyla's uncombed hair.

"He wouldn't have. We've only just met. He said…" She'd just met Josh. Her best friend had a tense relationship with him. Maybe there was a reason for that. Kyla had no proof he was a good guy beyond the butterflies in her stomach.

She bit back a groan and swallowed hard, unable to believe she'd made the same mistake again and allowed herself to fall for someone who lied and cheated.

"Oh, honey." Tasha's condescension grated like sandpaper on Kyla's ears. "I don't feel he's been truthful with you."

Kyla opened her mouth to speak but realized she had nothing to say. She felt so stupid. Dammit. That upstairs had been her rebound sex. She thought she'd finally found herself after Alan, but it seemed like Josh had lured her into the exact same situation—using her for his enjoyment without any consideration for her feelings. To think she'd contemplated talking him out of his "no strings" arrangement.

"You know what? I'll call him down, and you can sort this out with him." Kyla stalked to the base of the stairs and hollered up, "Josh. You have company." Not the way she planned to wake him.

She looked back at Tasha, who had taken the cleared doorway as an invitation. She sat on the same sofa Kyla and Josh had made out on, with their clothing still scattered around her. She crossed her legs and plucked Kyla's bra from between a couch cushion with two fingers.

Kyla had to get out. She couldn't keep looking at Natasha, couldn't stand how Kyla imagined Josh would look at either of them.

Thankfully, Josh's sweatshirt hung on the coat stand by the door. She slipped it on with shaking fingers and leashed Thor, who'd padded obediently to her side. With a deep, steadying breath, she turned to face the woman who had ruined her afternoon.

"He should be right down." Kyla opened the door as Josh's footsteps sounded on the stairs.

"Kyla? What—"

She froze but refused to look at him. "I'm taking Thor for a walk."

Josh fell silent for a long moment, then groaned. "Oh, for fuck's sake." More footsteps. A hand on her wrist. "Kyla. Don't go."

"Come on, Thor."

Kyla wrenched her wrist away from Josh and hurried out the door as gracefully as possible.

"Honey, you can get dressed first," Tasha called after her, amusement lacing her voice.

As the door closed behind her, Kyla let her tears fall.

CHAPTER SEVENTEEN

Josh blinked. He'd just woken from a deep sleep—the best sleep he'd had in a long time after the best sex he'd ever had. His tired brain struggled to follow the string of events that led to Kyla storming out and his lying, cheating ex sitting on his couch with her chin up like a goddamn princess as if she had every right to be there.

"Tasha? What the hell?" Josh scrubbed a hand across his face and turned toward her even though he knew he should go after Kyla.

"I missed you, baby." Tasha slid her fingertips down her neck, batting her lashes and twirling her blonde hair around her finger. Josh's stomach roiled. Those moves used to work on him. A couple of cute little gestures and his brain would turn from fighting to fucking in a moment. Now, it had no effect. He'd fallen for that angelic act for the last six months, but as recently as a few days ago, so had other men. Maybe what led to Tasha's arrival didn't matter as much as the furious heat that had started to build in his chest.

"It looks like you missed me, too." She looked pointedly

down at his boxers. Josh suddenly remembered waking up excited and hoping for a round two before Kyla's hollering.

"Jesus." Josh found his damp shorts on the floor by the sofa and yanked them on. He'd already forgotten how difficult Tasha made arguments. "What the hell are you doing here?"

"You didn't come home for the last two nights." She sucked her full bottom lip into her mouth. "Why didn't you tell me you were still coming to the cabin? I would have come with."

Josh's mouth fell slightly open. He ran his fingers through his hair and tugged. He couldn't get the image of Tasha riding another man out of his head. She couldn't just blow past that with a few winning smiles.

"Are you kidding me? I didn't think I had to spell this out for you, but we're not together anymore, Tasha. Hell, I'm starting to feel like we never were. The last six months seem like a big damn lie to me."

He glanced through the window next to the door, but Kyla had already disappeared into the woods. He gritted his teeth. How long had she been alone with Tasha?

Tasha crossed her arms and pouted. God, were her lips fake too? "I don't know what you're talking about, baby."

"You don't remember Eric? You seemed to know him pretty damn well the other night." Josh ran his hand over his chest, over his heart that, despite his better judgment, still hurt.

Tasha sighed, but it sounded more aggrieved than regretful. "Baby, I can explain."

"I don't want to hear it, Tash! Nothing you can say is gonna make this better." Josh took a shaky breath and tried to rein in his temper. Yelling wouldn't get her out of there any faster, no matter how good it felt. "You can't explain away screwing another man. You just can't. We're done."

"But you didn't even talk to me about it." She stood and put her hands on her hips. "And who was that woman in her underwear? Maybe *I* should be upset. It looks like you've already moved on. Did you even care about me at all?"

A moment ago, Josh had been angry. When Tasha mentioned Kyla, he became furious.

"Fuck you." His voice sounded cold.

Tasha smiled and took a step closer. "She sure left in a hurry. She's obviously not interested in you like I am."

He looked out the window. Kyla's car sat in the driveway. She couldn't have gotten far without it. Thank god for small miracles. He could fix this. He couldn't let Kyla believe whatever lies Tasha probably fed her.

He couldn't let her think he'd made her the other woman.

"I don't know how to be any clearer. Get out of my house."

Tears welled up in her beautiful eyes. "Joshy, baby. Please give me another chance. You didn't show up for our date. I was lonely."

"Don't do this." He found his shirt in a puddle of rainwater on the coffee table but pulled it on anyway. "And for the love of god, don't come back."

Tasha's black makeup streaked down her cheeks, and she seemed to crumple in on herself. Just two days ago, seeing her cry would have prompted a dozen roses and a dinner out. Now, Josh understood the tears were just another part of her act.

He stepped closer, and she looked at him with hopeful eyes. Josh avoided her gaze and placed a steady hand on her shoulder to lead her out. He couldn't take any chances she'd try and pull him in with her tricks. She sulked down the driveway and whimpered when he slammed the door of her BMW behind her.

Josh looked up at the sky and took another shaky breath. The clouds had begun to clear, and the late-afternoon sun shone bright. Only puddles remained as proof of the after-noon's storm. As Tasha departed, his temper started to cool, and worry flooded in to take its place. Kyla had no experience in the woods, and night approached all too quickly. All sorts of animals prowled the park.

In the back of his mind, a little voice pointed out that he wasn't normally the worrying type. He ignored that while praying she hadn't gotten too far.

CHAPTER EIGHTEEN

KYLA STUMBLED THROUGH THE WOODS, HER EYES BURNING. SHE should've grabbed her car keys. She should've grabbed pants. She should've stabbed Josh Hamilton that first day he'd frightened her and never looked back. How stupid. Clearly, her best friend didn't talk to his brother because Josh was a selfish liar, and she should've realized instead of being drawn in by expressive eyes and chiseled abs.

Thor barked and urged Kyla forward. She followed him without thought. She didn't know what poison ivy looked like, exactly. Worse, she didn't know if bears liked the smell of sex. She had read somewhere that sharks were attracted to it.

God, she was out of her element. At least the rain had stopped.

"K-Kyla?"

Kyla's heart jumped to her throat at the sound of a voice. She whirled around to see Tiff, one of Josh's friends she'd met by the waterfall. Thor barked and started his wiggle-wag to greet the woman.

"Hi. So, uh, how about that rain?" Kyla flushed and kicked herself for her total lack of normal communication skills.

"That was crazy." She chuckled, but her appraising gaze never left Kyla. "You guys make it down okay?"

Kyla blushed harder at the memory of Josh carrying her and what came after. "We did, thanks."

Tiff nodded thoughtfully. If Kyla didn't know any better, she'd say the woman looked worried. "So, are you and Josh…"

Kyla flinched. "I'm Dylan's best friend."

Tiff quirked a brow. "Ah. How's Dylan doing? I haven't seen him in years."

Kyla crossed her arms over her chest. Despite the sun, the rain had cooled off the summer day. "He's great. A detective with the Missoula Police Department."

A moment of silence passed between the two women. Tiff seemed to be wrestling with something.

"Are you okay?" Tiff finally asked.

Kyla's eyes stung again. "I'm not sure."

"Do you wanna come in?" She pointed to a retro log cabin just two houses down. "I'm over there, and you look like you could use some company."

Kyla trained her gaze on Thor. Company sounded heavenly. She just had to swallow these emotions first. "I had to get out of there."

"Totally." Tiff smiled and offered a hand. "I've got spare sweats in my bag if you want."

"You know what? That might be a good idea." Kyla laughed, and she hoped Tiff didn't notice the sound was thick with unshed tears.

* * *

THOR DOZED AT HER FEET, AND THE FIRE CRACKLED WITH WARMTH. SHE had reached a level of solace she hadn't realized she'd sought. This moment, sitting by the fire, the smell of wood smoke soaking into her clothes, surrounded by trees with new friends beside her, would stay with her after she left these woods.

The only thing she wanted, she realized with a sour taste in her mouth, was Josh. She missed his easy laughter, his intense eyes, and the comfort of his body pressed against hers.

She closed her eyes and allowed herself to think of the man who'd had his hands on her skin, his mouth on her body, and his cock inside her only two hours ago. She shivered at the memory. Having him just once, to help each other forget, had seemed like an incredible idea before it happened—before she realized he wasn't the man she thought he was.

Nonetheless, she'd had him, and she struggled not to want more. She craved his arms around her and his kiss on her neck behind her ear. Josh Hamilton would be a difficult man to forget.

"You want a hotdog?"

Kyla opened her eyes at the sound of Chad's voice. He held four sticks with hotdogs on the ends. She laughed. "I would love one."

She accepted a stick and, following Chad's example, held it over the flames. "I've never done this before."

"What?" He placed one hand over his heart. "How repressed was your childhood?"

"Very."

He nudged her shoulder with his, laughed, and turned his hotdog over. In a quieter voice, he said, "Look, Josh has been one of my best buddies since I was seven, but if you don't feel safe over there, you are more than welcome here for the night."

Kyla hesitated. Did she feel unsafe with Josh? Hurt, certainly. Maybe even devastated. But when she pictured his eyes, she didn't feel unsafe. Her hot dog dipped a little as her grip on the stick loosened, and it instantly caught fire.

She yanked her burning hotdog back and blew it out with a

wry chuckle. "Thank you. But... I don't think that's going to be necessary."

"Does this have anything to do with the little robe you showed up in?" Jer asked from across the fire.

"I'm glad it's dark, so you can't see me blush."

"I can see it," Chad crowed.

"So, this is where the party is," declared a masculine voice from around the corner of the cabin. A figure stepped out, shadowy and difficult to distinguish. Kyla's blood ran cold.

Thor barked, jumped up, and ran over to the guest. He stepped into the firelight, and Kyla shot out of her chair.

Dylan.

Her already burnt hot dog fell into the firepit, and her face flushed hotter. "Oh, shoot. Dammit."

Nothing about Dylan had changed since the last time she saw him, but something about the air between them felt different. He looked at her with the awareness of a lover, not a best friend. He'd set his shoulders protectively, possessively. She couldn't sense any of the comfort she had always enjoyed in his presence.

Her heart broke in an instant. He wasn't over the kiss. That stupid kiss born of nothing but stress, fear, and loneliness.

My god. She had ruined everything.

Kyla cleared her throat.

"Hey, Rosy." Dylan smiled at her before he pulled her into a bear hug. Then he kissed the top of her head.

As he held her, that little ball of guilt from earlier roared up in her chest and consumed her like a tidal wave. Not telling him about Josh felt like lying, but she barely wanted to admit she'd slept with his brother, much less that he'd seduced her and made her the other woman. She didn't want to see a Hamilton. She didn't want to unpack the roiling mixture of guilt, shame, and hurt in front of a bonfire full of people who knew she'd been running around the woods in lingerie.

"Hey, Dill." She stood on her toes to kiss his cheek. "What are you doing out here?"

"What, I can't come to check on my best friend?" He finally let her go and reached down to pet Thor.

She bit her lip. Something in his eyes looked strange, almost tense. Had something happened with Alan? Dylan wouldn't have ignored the fact she'd told him not to come without a good reason.

"Kyla, here." Tiff passed her another hotdog.

She smiled, grateful for the distraction. "Are you sure you trust me with this?"

"It's a hotdog. You'll be fine," Jer said.

Kyla sat back down on the edge of the Adirondack chair to watch her roasting wiener and avoid Dylan's gaze. She could feel his attention on her and bit her lip. He had an uncanny knack for picking up on her mood.

She had never been uncomfortable around Dylan before. She couldn't be. She didn't want to be. They were best friends.

Her ears roared, and her hands shook as she listened to Dylan catch up with his childhood friends. She wanted to run. Running had become her MO.

But the cabin held Josh and Tasha, so unless she wanted to drive three hours back to Missoula, she had to face the feelings churning in her belly.

"What happened to you?" Dylan asked.

"What? What do you mean?"

"Something's wrong with your hair."

Kyla winced. Dead giveaway. Under normal circumstances, she'd never leave the house without at least scraping her curls back into a ponytail, but right now, her hair hung loose and tousled around her shoulders. She carefully did not think about how it became tousled.

"I'm roughing it, obviously." Kyla forced a casual smile.

"She and Josh were caught in the rain," Jer said.

She peeked at Dylan, and he frowned. "What were you doing in the rain?"

"Hiking."

He nodded slowly, his eyes still on hers. It felt like an entire silent conversation passed between them in mere seconds. He knew. He had to know. If her best friend couldn't tell she'd just opened her heart, soul, and body to his brother, even more was wrong with the world than she thought.

"Kyla. Your hotdog's burning," Tiff said.

She laughed awkwardly and looked back to the fire. Sure enough, another sausage was in flames. "It's fine. I'll eat it."

"You sure?" Chad asked. "You don't have to."

"No, I will."

"Kyla?" Her heart dropped. She recognized that voice instantly. Josh picked his way carefully from around the side of Chad's cabin.

"Hey," she called.

"Jesus, I'm sorry about that. Fuck, I had no idea—" He skidded to a stop when he saw Dylan. "Hey, bro. What are you doing here?"

"Why does no one want me here?" He laughed in true Dylan fashion, but it didn't sound like his usual, carefree laughter. He sounded guarded. Kyla ached to pull her knees into her chest, to become smaller.

Josh stepped closer and clapped his brother on the shoulder. "Is everything okay?" Josh asked. The tension between them was palpable, but Kyla didn't know if it came from the past or the very obvious present.

"I was following Kyla's ex and lost track of him. I thought he left town, so I figured I'd check in with her here."

Both brothers looked at her, and she dropped her head. Dylan had ignored her request for him to prioritize solving the case. Josh seemed to think *"fuck, sorry"* would make up for what he did. Exhaustion seeped into her bones.

She couldn't do...this. Whatever this ended up being. Not in front of these three strangers who had been so sweet to her. "I'm going back to the cabin."

"Kyla," Dylan said. "Wait."

She shook her head. "I'm just going to bed."

"It's seven o'clock," he said.

"I'm tired." She glanced at Josh, then turned her attention to Chad, Tiffany, and Jer. "Thanks for the entertaining evening, the burnt hotdogs, and...everything."

"Anytime." Tiff grinned.

Kyla brushed by Josh and took a moment to breathe in his scent. Unfortunately, that would have to be the last time. He reached for her hand, but she slid it from his grasp and glanced back at Dylan. He narrowed his eyes, and she felt like a child with her hand caught in the cookie jar.

She hurried back to Josh's place as her stomach churned, guilt, humiliation, and regular old nausea promising to keep her up all night. At least no one seemed to be following her.

A tear slipped down her cheek, and a desperate urge to laugh bubbled in her throat. Maybe she'd finally gone crazy because she *wanted* Josh to follow her. Nothing made her feel stupider, but they hadn't talked yet, and she desperately wanted to believe he had a good explanation. Maybe Tasha had been lying, or maybe Kyla had misunderstood. Either way, she couldn't take another heartbreak right now.

She reached the bottom of the driveway.

"Kyla."

She turned to Josh. He held out a large yellow flashlight and the keys to the cabin.

Kyla swallowed down the shy smile her heart wanted to offer him. He didn't deserve it. "Hey."

"I'll watch to make sure you get in safe."

She looked up at his face, so perfect in the sunset glow. "Thank you." Their hands brushed when she took the keys and the flashlight.

"Dammit, Kyla. We need to talk, but Dylan—"

Dylan. She shrugged. She couldn't deal with that now. "He says he can't find Alan, but I told him not to come up. He could have called."

Josh nodded. "I'm sorry—"

Kyla cut him off with a wave. "We'll talk later, okay? Enjoy this time with your friends."

Josh leaned in. The heat from his body tempted her. She wanted to feel his arms around her once more, but she harnessed her willpower and stalked back to the cabin.

CHAPTER NINETEEN

Josh waited on the road until Kyla unlocked the cabin door, glanced over her shoulder at him, then slipped inside. For a half-second, he really thought she would come back out and invite him inside. They needed to talk. Tasha had barely been able to admit that he'd dumped her, so it didn't seem like too much of a stretch she'd tell Kyla they were back together. He needed to put that right.

The door slammed behind her. The sound hit him like a slap in the face, and he knew that was how she intended it. He swallowed.

Kyla didn't need the complication of his ex. He understood that, but he thought he'd shown Kyla enough of himself that she wouldn't buy Tasha's story.

A lump built in his throat. The sex had been incredible, passion and humor wrapped into one. She'd fallen asleep first, and he'd stayed awake for a few extra moments just to look at her. He'd run a finger down her cheek, marveling at the softness, and drifted off to what felt like his best sleep in months. He couldn't just let Tasha sweep in and ruin that.

Josh kicked a rock in the driveway and tried not to swear

loudly enough to frighten her. He'd only promised no strings because he thought she'd want that. Josh remembered the set of her shoulders as she stalked out the door, the fire dancing in her eyes when he approached Chad's cabin. She had deeper feelings than he'd guessed.

After taking his frustration out on a few more innocent pebbles, Josh meandered back to the bonfire at Chad's place.

On top of everything else, now he had to deal with Dylan.

He didn't want Dylan here. Not now. Not when the looks between him and Kyla at the fire revealed history, maybe something more than friendship.

Sure, Dylan had been intense over the phone, but it sounded like he wanted to protect *her* heart.

Okay, that didn't even sound true in his head. He got the vibe Dylan had feelings, but Josh had no idea they were strong enough to drive all the way here in a goddamn rainstorm.

A look had passed over Dylan's face when Josh grabbed Kyla's hand, a look he hadn't seen for seven years. Possessiveness. Anger.

Josh could still remember the hazy, too-drunk feeling of looking up from a beautiful woman and seeing that expression on his brother's face.

Josh had been working so damn hard to make it up to Dylan, to prove their bond meant everything to him and that Dylan could trust him around the women in his life.

Except Kyla wasn't Ely. Josh didn't regret making love to her. He couldn't think of that as a mistake, and she'd kept insisting Dylan was her best friend and nothing more. Josh had believed her. He still did. Or he wanted to.

Dylan's feelings had to be one-sided.

Josh sighed, unable to figure out why she'd taken off. Clearly the Tasha thing bothered her, but some tension had also lingered with Dylan.

Fuck. These last few days had spiraled into the type of drama Josh had come up here to avoid.

"She get back safe?" Chad asked as Josh returned to the fire and took the seat across from his brother.

"Yeah. Safe and sound."

"So, what the hell is going on?" Dylan stared him down, eyes alight with the fire.

Josh rubbed the back of his neck as he tried and failed to meet his brother's gaze. "You know I came up here to get away and found out you offered the place to your buddy."

Dylan snorted.

Jer and Chad looked between the brothers like a tennis match.

"Kyla and I spent the last few days together, cooking and hiking. We really hit it off. Then Tasha showed up as if I would take her back."

"Wait. Are *you* dating Kyla?" Jer asked Dylan. Josh could kiss him. Maybe he'd get the answer to a question he didn't want to ask.

"No," Dylan said through gritted teeth.

"But?" Chad pointed the neck of his beer bottle in Dylan's direction. "Do you *wish* you were dating her?"

"I..." Dylan shrugged, staring at the ground. Josh had never seen him look so lost before. Dylan had always been the rock Josh could count on, especially after their mom died. "I don't know."

The skin on the back of Josh's neck prickled and sweat dampened his T-shirt. He didn't want to keep fighting with his brother, but he couldn't just walk away this time. He felt... something for Kyla. Something special. Josh didn't know if she felt the same, but he had to fight for her to find out.

"Fuck." He didn't want to hurt Dylan, but neither could he lie.

"What?" Dylan asked. His face and neck appeared red, but Josh couldn't tell if that came from anger or the glow of the fire. Either way, Dylan's expression had turned from hurt to pissed, as if he'd braced for a physical confrontation. Josh hoped their conversation wouldn't come to that. He'd lose, but he wouldn't run if Dylan decided to hit him.

"I like her," Josh said.

"Of course you do," Dylan said slowly. "She's the best."

"Not like that." Josh looked down at the fire, then back up at his brother. Finally, he met his gaze. "I think I have feelings for her."

"You *think*?" Dylan stood. "What the hell does that mean?"

"It means we had sex. And...it felt like more than just sex."

Dylan froze, his hands balled at his sides. The tendons in his neck bulged with unexpected rage. Josh knew the face his brother made when he wanted to punch him, but he'd never seen Dylan quite this furious before. Josh wanted to glance at the others to see if they were still there because they had gone completely silent, but he knew better than to look away from a man poised to fight.

"I told you to be careful with her," Dylan growled. "That she had just ended her engagement. That she was going through a hard time."

"I know." Josh gripped the arms of his camp chair.

"But what? You were thinking with your dick, so to hell with her feelings?" Dylan's voice grew louder. He took a step closer.

"Hey." Josh put his hands up, palms out. "It wasn't one-sided."

"Fuck you, Josh. You can't use that excuse whenever you sleep with the wrong woman." Dylan loomed another step closer.

Suddenly, Josh became very tired. He'd been having the same argument with Dylan for almost a decade, and he couldn't remember the last time he'd felt so emotional about a girl. He just wanted to go home and smooth things over with Kyla. He sighed heavily. "I'm going to bed. Feel free to stay on the couch."

With that, he stood and headed back to the cabin. Behind him, Chad said, "Hey, take a second. Calm down." There was a small scuffle of wood chips that Josh could only guess meant Chad or Jer had pushed Dylan back into his chair. Josh didn't even consider turning around.

He hoped Kyla would let him in when he knocked. More than that, he hoped he could tell her what he'd just told Dylan.

CHAPTER TWENTY

A shower hadn't eased the chill in Kyla's bones, so she hoped comfort food would do the trick. She sat cross-legged under a quilt on the sofa in sweatpants and a T-shirt, alternately stuffing her face with a messy sandwich and potato chips.

She had wanted to eat her first hotdog ever cooked over a fire. She had wanted to enjoy rebound sex with a hot guy. Hell, she'd wanted to enjoy a relaxing week in the goddamn woods, but it seemed she wouldn't be getting anything she wanted any time soon.

If only she could rewind the day to when she lay in bed with Josh, playing her fingers through the soft hair over his pecs and tasting the rainwater on his skin.

Before Natasha had made her feel like dirt. Before Dylan had decided that seeing her ranked higher than solving the break-in. Before Josh had let her walk into the house without him.

A knock sounded at the front of the cabin. Kyla glanced at the door, then back at her meal. It could be Josh, Dylan, Tiff, Natasha, or, at this point, even Alan, and she didn't think she could deal with most of them.

She ate one more chip, then sighed, untangled herself from

the quilt, and strode to the front door. She had the only keys, after all. Through the window, she spotted Josh with a small, pink wildflower in his hand and an apologetic look on his face.

Maybe she could deal with him. Kyla unlocked and opened the door but didn't step out of the doorway.

"You're back early." Barely half an hour had passed since she'd left the bonfire. Its light still flickered through the trees.

Josh grimaced slightly. "No fun without you."

Kyla's heart fluttered. She had to stay strong. "So, you figured a flower would be enough to win me over?"

Josh looked down at the slightly wilted bloom in his hand. "Seemed better than showing up empty-handed."

A moment of silence hung in the air. Kyla refused to tell him what to say. Either he cared enough to figure it out, or she'd wasted her time.

"I... I'm sorry," Josh said. "Tasha lied or refused to see what was right in front of her. I technically never told Tasha she and I were finished. Therefore, I'm sorry. You didn't deserve that."

Kyla searched his eyes. Josh stared back at her without hesitation. She swallowed. Could she really let someone get close enough to hurt her that badly again? Kyla remembered the look on Josh's face when she'd found his tattoo this afternoon.

She plucked the flower from his hand and stepped back. A wide grin split Josh's face as he stepped in. His arm brushed hers, and her belly flipped at the contact.

He observed the remains of her dinner. "What are you eating?"

"Chips and a sandwich. Want some?"

"Yes."

She led the way back to the sofa where, only hours before, they had decided to take that next step. She wanted to cuddle up to his chest. Instead, she left space between them and pulled the blanket back up around her.

"What kind of sandwich did you make?"

"A bunch of cold cuts. Cheese. Honey mustard."

Josh reached for the other half of the sandwich and took a bite. "Mm. It's so gross it's kind of good."

"So..." Kyla had no idea what to say. Too much had happened. Too much darkened the space she'd left between them.

Josh turned to face her. "Nothing's changed about the way I feel about you."

Kyla met his gaze. "How's that?"

"I like you."

She couldn't help the grin that tugged at her lips. "I like you, too."

"And I want you. Again."

She could hear it coming. "But?"

"I think we should talk, you know?"

She wanted to laugh with him, relax and eat and tease each other. But they couldn't because, apparently, real life could reach them even three hours away.

"What do you want to talk about?" she asked.

"I want you to know"—he leaned over to set the half-eaten sandwich back on the plate—"I made it clear to Tasha that it's over between her and me. Officially. Somehow, me storming out while she fucked another man didn't clarify that."

"Good." Kyla studied him. Josh wrinkled his brow in frustration, but his eyes exuded an exhaustion that told her this afternoon had been just as hard for him. She needed more, though. She wanted to understand. "What happened back in Missoula?"

"You really want to hear about that?" he asked.

Kyla shrugged. "If you're willing. I mean, it might help me to see the full picture."

"All right." Josh rubbed his hands on his jeans. "I was supposed to meet Tasha for dinner. I was late. Work. You get it."

She nodded.

"She wasn't at the restaurant when I arrived."

Anger rose in Josh's voice. He couldn't fake that. She knew it too well. He'd been betrayed, and the betrayer had the nerve to show up as if she belonged. She even treated Kyla as though she were the outsider. Her own anger rose to meet his.

Kyla tightened the blanket around her. "Where was she?"

"Her place." Josh pressed his lips together. "With another man. Moaning, screaming, the whole shebang." He laughed, then shook his head. "Live pornography, starring my girlfriend."

Kyla laughed with him. She didn't find any of this funny, but she knew that heartbreak, that feeling of disloyalty, and sometimes laughter really helped, especially when you had someone to commiserate with.

For the first time since Tasha knocked on the door, the tension in her shoulders decreased.

Josh had a way of seeing the silver lining in everything. More than that, he knew how to make her smile. In only three days, he understood her.

"Did you know the guy? Please tell me he wasn't your best friend," Kyla asked.

"No. The tale is thankfully not that tragic. I don't know anyone named Eric. But I did see his dick, and goddamn, I don't get the appeal."

Kyla laughed. "I think it depends on the man."

"Yeah?" Josh smiled widely. "What about me? Did I pass the test?"

"You passed with flying colors." Although she wouldn't be opposed to having another look.

Josh leaned forward. "I really am sorry, Kyla. I'm sorry

Tasha came up here at all, and I'm sorry for everything she said."

"She's kind of a bitch, to be perfectly honest. But…" Kyla weighed her next words carefully in light of his honesty. "I don't think you need to apologize for things she did."

"Thank you." Josh shook his head. "I don't know what I saw in her."

"I do," Kyla said. "She's stunning."

"What can I say?" Josh closed the gap between them and ran his fingers through her hair before stroking his thumb over her jawline. "I guess my type is beautiful women."

"But—"

He raised a brow. "But you still feel bad for leaving without confronting me first?"

Kyla shook her head and punched him lightly in the arm. "That's for interrupting."

"Right. Sorry." Josh's smile was wide, easy. "You were saying?"

God, how she wished she could tell him how she truly felt at that moment—that she had feelings for him, feelings far deeper than the scorching sexual connection they shared. Those feelings were the reason she had taken off at first glimpse of his ex. If she could truly handle a one-night stand with Josh, finding his ex-girlfriend at the door shouldn't have bothered her.

But it had.

A lot.

Natasha's arrival felt like a wake-up call, making her realize how much she wanted Josh. Though wary, Kyla was ready to allow him into her life. If he wanted her. She met his eyes. The intensity of his gaze warmed her cheeks and woke her heart.

"I'm sorry for leaving when Tasha showed up. I'm sorry for stealing your sweatshirt and running away into the wilderness without pants or an explanation."

"Apology accepted. Why did you, though?" Concern pinched his face. "Leave when Tasha showed?"

"Isn't it obvious?" She stepped on paper-thin ice. The truth bubbled on her lips.

"I think so." Josh nodded. His eyes showed a mixture of caution and desire. Her stomach swooped. She could only come up with one explanation for his caution. He'd guessed she wanted more, and he only wanted a vacation hook-up.

He opened his mouth to speak.

"Listen, Josh." She cut him off before he could let her down gently. "There's more we have to talk about."

"I agree." Instead of talking, he leaned in and, after making sure she didn't lean away, pressed a soft kiss to her lips. When she hummed, Josh ran his tongue across her bottom lip. Shivers cascaded down her body.

"Josh." Though it killed her, she braced both hands on his broad chest and shoved. She would never be able to think with his mouth so close.

"Sorry. I'm easily distracted."

So was Kyla. She could easily sink into his big, gorgeous blue eyes and happily drown. Josh Hamilton had to be one of the most handsome men she'd ever met, but she had to act tough, or she would never be able to resist that face. Those dimples. "Where was I? Oh yes. Dylan."

Kyla tried to see Dylan's point of view, but being an only child left her without a reference point. If Dylan had a one-night stand with Andrea, Kyla could only imagine worrying about whether he would remember to call Andrea after or having to choose sides in a breakup.

Josh dropped his head back on the sofa. "Do we have to?"

"He's been there for me through break-ins and breakups. Your brother is my best friend."

Josh sighed. "He used to be mine, too."

Kyla dropped her head back next to his, remembering the weird look on Dylan's face. "He was acting off tonight."

He snorted. "That's an understatement. After you left the fire, he got worse."

She grabbed his hand and squeezed. "I'm sorry. Do you think it was because of me? Because of us?"

Josh sat up, wrapped her in his arms, and kissed her temple in a gesture so sweet, she could have cried. "Don't worry. We'll sort this out."

"I am worried, though." She'd never even fought with Dylan before. The closest they'd come was a few months of bickering about whether he should get a dog, which she'd won when Thor flunked K9 training.

When Josh pulled back, his smile looked tight and didn't reach his eyes. "This isn't on you, okay?"

"Isn't it, though?" she asked. "Dylan's here because of Alan."

Josh shook his head. "I wish. Dylan is here because he's in love with you. I didn't know until I saw the way he looked at you tonight."

The bottom fell out of Kyla's stomach. Dylan couldn't be in love with her. That wasn't possible. He was her best friend, basically her brother. She couldn't lose him to something as stupid as this.

"I don't believe you," Kyla said.

Josh sat back slightly and studied her. Her stomach churned unhappily. Dylan had made a bad joke about the kiss in that email, but he couldn't be in love with her because then she would have ruined everything by falling for his brother.

Josh crossed his arms. "He basically said so himself."

Kyla laughed, feeling slightly hysterical. "He's my best friend. We share Thor, watch crappy TV, and eat junk food. I vent to him like I would a girlfriend."

"Is it wrong for me to be jealous of that?" Josh asked. "Of the time you've spent with him?"

"Yes." Kyla made eye contact with Josh as she spoke. "Dylan and I are just friends."

She just needed to tell Dylan the same thing and ensure he heard her. She could not, would not lose him. A little open communication would fix everything. She'd just pull him aside the next time she saw him.

"Okay." Josh nodded. "I did tell him about...us. And he tried to kick my ass."

Kyla sighed and dropped her head into her hands. "He's upset. I'm sorry that landed on you. But we're not together, Dylan and me. Not that...you know, you and I are." Unless she got her way, that was.

Josh traced a slow pattern of circles over the back of her shirt. "Yeah, well, guys aren't always logical."

He could say that again. If his touches were anything to go by, Josh seemed to be struggling to keep things between them to one night as well. Kyla didn't want to play games. She wanted Josh, and she would make damn sure he knew that.

"I'm sorry Dylan's hurting, and I'll talk to him, but I don't want you and me to end yet." She pressed her lips against his mouth and moved to straddle him. She wanted to take his hand and pull him up to the bedroom to have the round two she'd fantasized about since she woke up.

Before she could make her move, the front door swung open, and Dylan stepped inside.

CHAPTER TWENTY-ONE

Josh should have locked the front door. His brother stared at him with a burning rage in his eyes and his mouth slightly open.

However, Josh knew him. Dylan's pride had been wounded, and under the rage lay hurt. Josh wanted to say he felt bad, but Kyla was quickly becoming someone he was willing to hurt people to keep.

"Dylan." Kyla tried to stand up, but Josh held her close. Something in his heart he didn't care to investigate ached at the thought of her going to Dylan. Maybe he needed her as a shield so his and Dylan's fight wouldn't come to blows.

Thor barked and ran to greet them, and Kyla leaned over to kiss his head. Dylan slammed the door behind him, and Kyla flinched, almost losing her balance on Josh's lap. Josh tightened his hold.

"Kyla," Dylan said evenly. "Can you give Josh and me a minute alone? Please?"

She looked back at Josh and pulled her hand from his. She looked mad, and he hoped to hell Dylan was the target this time. She rose, crossed the room to Dylan, wrapped her arms around his neck, and stood on her toes to whisper in his ear. Josh would have given anything to know what she said to Dylan. When Kyla said she'd talk to him, did that mean she'd remind him she and Dylan were just friends? Or now she knew how Dylan felt about her, would she change her mind and ultimately pick him over Josh?

Dylan smiled, which made Josh jealous. Fuck.

Kyla walked up the stairs, Thor on her heels. Josh didn't want to begin the conversation. Neither did Dylan, it seemed. A moment of tense silence passed as Dylan crossed his arms and leaned against the wall.

Josh stood and put his hands up. "Listen—"

"No, Josh, you listen. I gave you one instruction: stay away. But listening has never been your strong suit, has it? She's my life right now. Dammit, I love her. I'm not giving her up for you or anyone."

"There's gonna come a point when you realize I'm not a kid anymore, and you don't get to just go around handing out orders." Josh reached up to yank at his hair. "You said she was your friend. You said stay away. I *tried*, but there's something unavoidable between us. Hell, she made the first move!"

Dylan paced to the kitchen island and back. "Unavoidable. Ha. I'll start treating you like an adult when you start acting like one, not some two-bit, star-crossed Romeo. Did she tell you we kissed? The night before she left? We were on the way to something."

Josh flinched. No, she hadn't mentioned the kiss, but she had sworn up and down she and Dylan were just friends. Maybe the kiss had been bad. Maybe she deserved a little benefit of the doubt. Josh took a deep breath.

"She didn't give me that vibe, Dylan." He shrugged. "She told me, she assured me, there was nothing between you two."

"But you've already fucked her. You didn't even give me a

chance to find out." Dylan looked over at the stairs, then back at Josh. "This is Sky all over again. I need to realize you're not a child? You keep screwing up in the same stupid, childish ways. I just—

"I didn't fuck her, Dylan." Josh paused. He had to be certain. "I fell for her. The sex was just part of that."

Storm clouds brewed on Dylan's face. He took an uneven breath through his teeth. Josh had never seen his brother this angry, even when he'd spilled coffee on his laptop during finals week, even at the campfire before. In total silence, Dylan turned and threw a punch at the wall behind him. His hand rocketed through the long window next to the door. Glass shattered. Josh lunged forward. Upstairs, Thor began barking.

"Dyl—" Josh extended his hands, approaching his brother as he would a wild animal.

"Don't." Dylan looked at his bleeding knuckles, covered in glass. "I'll stay with Jer."

Thor pounded down the stairs to investigate the crisis.

"You don't have to—"

Dylan grabbed Thor's leash, then slammed the door behind him.

"Dammit." Josh sat down and dropped his head back on the sofa. He closed his eyes to try to shut out the pain, confusion, and unjustness of the entire situation.

Footsteps approached. He opened his eyes, then widened them at the sight of Kyla standing in front of him, her flannel robe gaping open to expose a pink lace bra and panty set. Her pale skin looked like porcelain, and her rosy nipples peeked through the sheer fabric. He struggled to hold back a groan of desire.

Any other day, he would have pulled her down on top of him and kissed her until they both fought for breath. But right now...

"Are you okay?" Her voice sounded quiet, unsure.

"Honestly, Kyla, I don't know."

She sat down on the couch, about five feet away from him. Out of reach. Gooseflesh covered her body, and her eyes were wide and red. "I'm sorry." She stared down at her hands on her lap. "I shouldn't have let things go as far as they did with us."

"What?" Josh sat up. Had what Dylan said changed things for Kyla? Did she wish she'd chosen Dylan now she knew how he felt about her? His brother had always been the one people trusted and gravitated toward. God, against Dylan, Josh didn't stand a chance. He scrubbed a hand across his face. "Do you regret having sex with me?"

"No, of course not, but—"

"But?" Agitated, he stood and began to pace. God, he needed some fresh air. "But, Kyla?"

"I've come between you and Dylan. I never meant to hurt you." She swiped a tear from her cheek, and his heart broke for her. Then, he heard what she was saying. She never meant to hurt *him*.

She'd already chosen, and he'd already lost. He strode to the door, spotted his keys, and grabbed them. He couldn't think with her in front of him. He opened his mouth to speak, then closed it. He didn't have anything to say. He opened the door, stepped outside, and shut it behind him. Clearly, she didn't have anything to say either.

The moonlight outlined his Jeep in the driveway. He wanted to scream, run, or go back inside and fuck the girl who stole his heart and ripped it out at the same time.

Josh opened the car door and slid inside. Dylan's bloody hand would haunt him for the rest of his days. He slammed his palm on the steering wheel. Dylan's accusatory tone and Kyla's tears would keep him up at night.

"Dammit."

Thunder rumbled overhead. If he had his wallet, he would have started the car and headed back to the city. He slumped over the steering wheel. It would be so easy to blame Kyla. To get mad, leave, and go back to running a bakery by himself. She could be a blip on his radar. Dylan would never forgive him, so Josh didn't have to worry about seeing them together.

Or it would have been easy three days ago.

He'd been alone, basically, since Dylan disappeared from his life seven years ago. He had a friend in Romeo, but that was more of a business relationship, a string of girlfriends who never made much of an impact, and his father, who never called. Josh had gotten used to the routine of quiet and careless, chance encounters. However, Kyla had woken something in him he hadn't even known existed. He'd spent at least half the last three days taking care of a girl he'd just met. With her also came Dylan and a chance to get his brother back.

Josh wanted that. He wanted everything. He'd been lonely for a long time without ever even realizing it.

He had to go back in and fight for Kyla, whatever that entailed.

A knock sounded on the passenger side window. The door opened, and Kyla leaned in. Her hair flowed like satin over her shoulders while her gaping robe gave him an incredible view of her breasts. "Can I come in?"

His smile came easily. "If you want to sit with an asshole."

"I don't think you're an asshole." She climbed into the cab, flashing a milky white inner thigh and more of her chest when the robe caught under her ass and pulled further open.

After she readjusted the robe, he turned in his seat to face her. "So."

She sighed and closed her eyes. "I'm sorry."

Josh braced himself. "I really like you, Kyla. I'd like to keep having you in my life, whichever way you'll let me do that. So, let's just pull off the bandage. You want to be with Dylan, right?"

Kyla opened her eyes and stared at him blankly for a moment. "What?"

Josh smiled ruefully. "I don't actually have that many friends, and I get why you'd want to date him now. You know how he feels."

"Josh, I..." Kyla blinked. "Finding out about Dylan's feelings doesn't change anything. I don't feel the same way. I told you that."

"But Dylan told me you kissed, and—"

"I know. I didn't want to eavesdrop, but the cabin isn't particularly soundproof. The thing is, Dylan didn't lie. We kissed for the first time a few days ago. I was upset when it happened, looking for comfort, but it was wrong. He's my friend. Then when you and I met, everything else fell away. There couldn't be anyone else." She pushed her long hair over her shoulder. "Josh, I don't know what else to tell you, except I don't have romantic feelings for him." Kyla set her hand over her heart.

"He does have feelings for you, though." Josh felt like he was going in circles. What did this mean for Kyla and him? Did it mean anything?

"I don't want to get in the way of your relationship with Dylan, but I don't want what we shared to be a one-night stand," she said, holding the robe closed.

"I don't want that either."

"Should I go?" A tear slid down her cheek. "I can leave in the morning."

Panic seared through Josh's veins. "No, Kyla. Fuck. I don't want you to leave. I want you to come."

They looked at each other, and though desire burned on Kyla's face, she smiled. "That was good."

Josh choked out a laugh. "This isn't funny."

"I know, but I want you, too. Maybe we need to do this one more time. You know, to make sure it's...worth it?"

"This?"

"Have sex."

Josh leaned in to take her mouth with his. He didn't know if his brother would ever forgive him, but at that moment, all he could think of was the woman in front of him, how much he wanted her, and how much it turned him on that she wanted him just as much.

Josh wished he had turned on the heat, but his hands were too busy to find the ignition. He caressed and warmed Kyla's chilled skin, teasing the most alluring sounds from her, sounds that vibrated over his lips and made each kiss that much better.

"You're freezing. We should go back inside." Josh's lips lingered a breath away from hers.

"Warm me up then." She wound her hands into his hair. "And I'm not talking about the heater."

Josh didn't need her to beg. If Kyla wanted him, she had him.

"You are perfection." He whispered those words against the skin between her breasts, over her heart.

She ran her fingers over his stubbled jaw. "You make me feel that way."

Kyla lay back on the seat and crooked her finger at him. She batted her lashes and puckered her pretty pink lips. She smiled, seductive and self-assured.

When they first met, she had been all flushed cheeks and innocence. He liked her sweetness, but this bold new attitude, obviously buoyed by his reassurance, was beyond erotic.

The soft fabric of her robe slipped off his temptress's shoulders, and she slid her arms free. Her breasts looked so full, and he wanted them in his mouth. He reached behind her back and unclasped the bra, pulling it down just enough and leaving her arms pinned to her sides. Her nipples stiffened in the cold, but Josh, ever the gentleman, quickly warmed them with hands and lips, sucking and pinching hard, wanting her to experience the intensity of his desire for her.

"More," she cried.

Josh glanced up. Her mouth had fallen open. Damn, he couldn't resist those lips. He had to taste them.

"You know what," he said. "You're too far away."

He hit the lever to put the seat into a reclined position, then crawled over the stick shift and spread himself on top of her. She spread her legs, then wrapped them around his hips. When he pushed his erection against her, she gasped, then rolled her hips, moaning at the friction. It seemed she didn't want to be patient, either. He nipped at her lip, her jaw, and that soft little place under her ear.

"Wait," he groaned. The heat radiating off her had him on the verge of release. He needed a minute to gain some control.

Kyla shook her head. "I don't want to."

Well, if she didn't want to wait....

Josh slid off the bottom of the seat and onto his knees in the footwell as he pushed her legs up onto the dashboard. The plastic of the glovebox jabbed into his back, but he didn't care —anything for her.

With a wolfish smirk, he sank his teeth into the waistband of her underwear and dragged them down. As the cool air hit her, she shivered, and again when he hooked his arms under her legs. Then he sank his face into the apex of her thighs.

Josh pressed his tongue into her, hard, over and over, with a relentless rhythm. Kyla's breath escaped her beautiful mouth in pants, whines, and a string of desperate moans that made his rock-hard erection even harder. Finally, her head fell back against the headrest.

"This is real." Kyla ran her hands through his hair. "Us. What I feel for you. How we work together."

"I agree." He glanced up at her flushed face and traced his thumb in circles around the sensitive peak of her breast. "Too hard?"

She grinned. "No such thing."

"Mm. We're going to get along just fine."

She pushed his head, wriggled out of his hands, and sat up. Gloriously naked, her hair fell in messy waves around her face, and a natural flush colored her cheeks. Josh could've stayed there, staring at her, forever.

Kyla smiled at him, then winked. "Let's go inside. Maybe you can build a nice toasty fire?"

"Yeah. That sounds good." Josh reached down between his legs to ease his discomfort. "Now?"

"Now." She laughed again, covered his hand with hers, and pressed a sweet, teasing kiss to the corner of his mouth. "I didn't say we were finished, but the seatbelt buckle is poking me in the back." She pulled the robe up and tied the belt tightly. "Plus, I have a wedding to shoot this coming weekend. I can't get sick."

Josh laughed and stole a kiss. "Your professionalism is turning me on."

Kyla opened the door of the Jeep and hopped out. The rain had returned, coming down in sheets. She let the summer shower soak her again. Like a rain goddess, she laughed and twirled on her bare toes.

"Come on," she yelled over the next clap of thunder, her hands held up as if she welcomed the downpour. "I can whisper business secrets in your car."

CHAPTER TWENTY-TWO

Kyla had never been the carefree girl who ran around in the rain, wearing nothing but a wet robe, who got to third base in a car with a man she hardly knew, who teased and flirted and laughed and felt entirely at ease in her skin.

The old Kyla, the Kyla of three days ago, would not have done any of that, but as she threw her head back in ecstasy and Josh kissed the pulse that pounded in her throat, something inside her had changed. Her heart raced, but she felt calm. In fact, she hadn't felt this relaxed since the break-in or her breakup.

She felt alive. Hope, joy, and certainty all swirled through her veins, pumped through her heart, and echoed in her ears. She pushed away the look on Dylan's face. She hadn't enjoyed herself with Josh to hurt Dylan. She couldn't let his moment of folly ruin her fun, her fresh start.

"You taste like the rain." Josh's words were a warm whisper, a breath of life on her cold skin.

Kyla slid her hand up the back of his neck. She tangled her fingers in the wet hair at his nape and anchored him to her body. Josh walked her backward and pinned her body against the old oak door, the same door she had angrily stormed out of earlier today, and he stripped away the one sorry scrap of fabric she had covering her body.

She stood naked outdoors in the middle of the night, just feet from neighboring cabins, and she didn't want to move. She didn't want him to stop.

Josh unlocked the door and, with one last kiss, opened it. Then he wrapped his arms around her shoulders, under her knees, and lifted her. She clung to his chest and kept her lips on his. He stepped carefully over the glass inside the door and through the living room, finally putting her down on top of the kitchen island. The marble cooled her naked body once again, but he soon warmed her with his hands and mouth.

"You're beautiful, Kyla." He moved his gaze over her exposed flesh. "I want you so much. I'll never get enough."

"You can have me." She pressed herself into him. "As many times as you want."

His jaw flexed. "Even after Tasha? After my brother?"

"Especially after that." A rush of confidence surged through her. "You picked me."

Josh offered her a smile so warm and genuine she shivered in delight, but then he stared at her naked body and replaced his smile with a cocky grin. Finally, he leaned down and kissed her stomach, then caressed her hips and thighs. She felt like he was taking her in, learning every curve and beauty mark, memorizing her skin.

Kyla sucked in a hard breath, then placed her hands on his shoulders. "Wait."

"What's wrong?" He cradled her ass with his hands.

"You want this, right? Us? No doubts."

Josh took her mouth in a hard kiss that left no question

unanswered. He unzipped his shorts, and they fell to his ankles. His hungry mouth muffled Kyla's groan. He pressed his firm, fit body against hers and devoured her, making Kyla feel like the most decadent dessert.

"We need a condom." Kyla couldn't wait anymore. She needed to feel Josh inside her.

Josh grinned. "Don't move."

He took off up the stairs, and she leaned back against the counter. She shivered without the heat of his body against hers, but Kyla had never felt so certain of anything in her life.

She wiped rainwater from her cheeks as Josh ran back down the stairs, naked and with the condom already on.

He traced shaky fingertips under her eyes. "You okay?"

"Yes." Kyla moved her fingernails over his bare chest, through the sexy dusting of hair, and over his tattoo.

He smoothed his hands across the tops of her thighs, then yanked them apart, pinning her legs against the counter. She gasped. The move screamed pure masculinity, dominant and demanding. Yet, despite the way he restrained her, Kyla felt protected, and when he ran the tip of his nose down her neck, she inhaled softly.

"You are so damn sexy, Kyla. No wonder I'm overexcited."

She pushed her chest out, seeking connection with his warm body. "You don't seem too overwhelmed."

He laughed softly and ran one hand up her side and back down. "I'm covering well." He licked her lips until she opened them for him, then rewarded her with a swirl of his tongue. "Your innocence is alluring. Your sweetness is everything."

Josh let go of her thighs so he could touch her breasts. She clamped her legs around him and drew her nails down his back. He hissed before he caressed the curve of her hip and pressed his hand to the back of her thigh.

Their groans sounded as one when Josh slid inside her, inch

by excruciatingly slow inch. The moment had started so lascivi-ous, so wanton that Kyla thought this would be a quickie—rough and fast against the counter, but Josh seemed to find passion in every moment. He liked to take his time, draw out her pleasure, and discover what set her alight.

Kyla wanted to say something sexy and alluring, but she could barely catch her breath. She also couldn't quite think straight. His hands seemed to be everywhere. He massaged her hips, stroked her sides, and grazed the curve of her breasts. He used his mouth, too. He suckled at her breasts to tease more moans and senseless words from her lips, and she defi-nitely had a hickey at the base of her throat, her first since college.

The sensations accompanying the slow friction between her legs were almost too much to bear. Yet, she didn't want him to stop. She didn't want this perfect moment to end.

"Come on, sexy girl." His gasp in her ear only fed the climax building inside her. She didn't know how Josh knew her body so well, so soon, but he seemed to hit that spot just right with every thrust. She dug her fingers into his flesh and dropped her head back as the intensity of the moment washed over her in waves. She cried out, coming so hard her vision blurred.

The stillness of Josh's hips and his stuttered breath told her he had fallen with her. His hot lips on hers made Kyla smile. "You are so damn beautiful," he said before kissing her again.

Kyla rested her head on his shoulder and spoke into the crook of his neck. "I will never get tired of doing that with you."

He laughed and buried his nose into her damp hair. "Is that an invitation to do it again?"

"I think so."

Josh laughed again. "You think so?"

She raised her head and met his gaze, expecting to find humor in his eyes. Instead, Kyla got lost in their intensity.

Josh opened his mouth to speak but closed it and pulled away from her body.

"What's wrong?" She crossed her arms, suddenly self-conscious.

He moved to the window and looked outside. "It's so dark, but I could have sworn I saw something. Someone."

CHAPTER TWENTY-THREE

"S*omeone's* *outside?*" K*yla* *drew* *her* *knees* *up* *to* *her* *bare* *chest.* "Who?"

He hated to see her nervous, so he shook his head. "I don't even know if I saw anything."

"Yes, you did, or you wouldn't have said anything."

"Honestly, it's too dark to really tell." He shrugged, trying to keep her calm. "Maybe it was just the rain?" Josh held out his hand, and she took it immediately. "Come on. Let's go upstairs and get dressed. Then I'll go outside and look around."

"What? You can't go outside alone." Kyla tightened her grip on his fingers.

"We're not in a horror movie." He tugged on her hand, and she hopped off the counter.

They climbed the stairs together, still naked, and he wished like hell he could enjoy the moment without checking every window. He knew the way trees moved here, and he knew he'd seen something else.

"What are you thinking?" she asked when they reached the bedroom.

He started slightly. He hadn't realized he'd been so obvious, but he didn't want to frighten her. "That I want to spend one freaking moment alone with you. No interruptions."

His admission made her smile, and he pressed her against the door to kiss her once more.

Bang.

That had definitely come from downstairs.

"Shit." Josh yanked open the door, raced to the dresser, and pulled on a pair of jeans and a T-shirt. "Will you wait here?"

"No." She followed him in and dressed in a sweatshirt and denim shorts. "I'm not going to sit here and get murdered." Kyla pulled her hair into a bun with a practiced hand.

Josh laughed humorlessly. "I just said we're not in a horror movie, didn't I?"

She rolled her eyes. "Mm. Let's go look." She headed out of the bedroom, and Josh jogged to catch up. "Do you have a base-ball bat or a golf club or something?"

"No," he said. "Just a flashlight."

"It *is* pretty heavy," she said, still two steps ahead of him on the stairs.

"Kyla." They reached the landing, and he grabbed her hand to stop her. "Let me go first, okay?"

"Fine." She paused to let him pass. He would have admired her bravery if he weren't so terrified for her safety.

Josh peeked around the corner to survey the kitchen and the living room. At first glance, he didn't see anyone. He'd locked the front door, but the patter of summer rain on the floor reminded him of the window Dylan had broken.

"See anything?" Kyla whispered.

"No." Josh padded down a few stairs and looked more closely.

Then the entire cabin went black.

"Fuck."

"Is that because of the storm?" Kyla asked. The unsaid "or" hung in the air.

Josh went back for Kyla and led her to the main floor, then looked out the window over the kitchen sink where he had previously seen movement. Chad's place still had light, and they fed from the same powerline. "Other cabins have power."

Kyla's arm brushed against his as she stood on her toes to peer through the window. "There. Someone's there." She pointed into the blackness behind the neighbor's place.

"I'm going to go outside and find out," he said.

"Josh, no. I know what you said, but this is every bad horror movie come to life."

He wrapped his arm around her shoulders and kissed her cheek. "I'll just go turn on the generator. Grab a knife and wait right here."

"Fine." Kyla had already turned toward the block where he kept his best butcher knife, the one she'd wielded against him before.

"It's gonna be all right, sugar," he said, then winced. Too early for pet names by far.

He strode through the dark cabin to where he last saw the flashlight by the front door and grabbed it. "Kyla?" he called into the darkness. "I'm going out the front. Okay?"

"Just hurry," she said. "And be careful."

Josh pulled on his jacket, popped the hood over his head, opened the door, and slipped out into the soaking summer night.

The side of the cabin had grown dark and muddy, and the rain had become a veritable downpour. His flashlight beam scanned over the wooded area between his and the Mackey's place, but he could barely see more than a foot ahead.

Movement to his left caught his eye.

"Hello?"

Thunder cracked overhead, then lightning. No one there.

Josh hurried to the generator on muscle memory. He didn't want to be outside in this storm longer than necessary. In the mountains, everything was extreme, especially the weather.

A branch snapped.

He straightened, put his back to the cabin, and waited for someone to come out from between the trees. Nothing. He turned back to the generator and prayed he could find the right switches. After a few tries, the lights flickered back on in the cabin, and Josh breathed a sigh of relief. Maybe something had gone legitimately wrong with the electricity. He would call the power company in the morning.

He took off toward the front of the cabin but ran square into what felt like a brick wall, except for the grunt on impact. Josh's flashlight scattered out of his hands, throwing a useless beam into the woods. He opened his mouth to yell, but before he could, a heavy fist cracked against his jaw.

Josh reeled back, seeing stars. In that second of hesitation, the attacker turned and stalked toward the house.

CHAPTER TWENTY-FOUR

Kyla sat with her back to the kitchen counter, a large butcher knife clutched in her sweaty hands. She tried to steel herself, but her hands wouldn't stop shaking. She didn't want to be the damsel in distress, but god, she felt like one.

She worried about Josh, too. She'd seen the way he went still, staring out the window. He wouldn't have done that if he hadn't seen something.

Natasha wouldn't come back in a thunderstorm, and Kyla didn't think Dylan would come in the back door or even return at all. Yes, he had broken things and stormed out, but he was emotionally upset. No matter how bad their relationship had gotten, he would never try to frighten her. She wouldn't believe that about Dylan. Not the man who trusted her with Thor, not the man who had her back when she was too afraid to sleep in her apartment alone after the break-in, not the man who kissed her.

Dammit. Dylan had feelings for her that he had not let on— and that broke her heart.

Kyla swallowed and tightened her grip on the knife. Barring a random mischief-maker, that left Alan.

How could a man who loved her once try to scare her like this?

He hadn't always been a monster. They'd loved each other once, and even if he couldn't manage to stay faithful to her, she couldn't fathom him going to these lengths. She didn't know what was more terrifying: a random intruder or a version of her ex she didn't know anymore.

The lights flicked back on, which only made her feel more exposed.

A knock echoed through the empty living room.

"Josh?" Her voice sounded shaky even to herself. He must have locked himself out.

A voice answered from outside, but the rain muffled the words.

She stood and crept across the room. It had to be Josh. What intruder would knock? The knife handle grew slick in her grasp as nervous sweat drenched her palms.

The knock came again, louder this time. She reached the front hall table, where Josh's keys should be. Empty.

That couldn't be Josh knocking.

She watched with growing horror as a large hand she recognized all too well reached through the shattered window and unlocked the door.

Alan.

Some instinct she didn't recognize sprang to life in her chest, and she sprinted the rest of the way across the room to throw her body against the door. If she could just keep it closed, nothing bad could happen. He'd have to leave. Josh would have to come back.

The doorknob turned against her ribs, and she pushed as hard as she could, digging her feet into the welcome mat. Kyla could hardly breathe. Slowly, inexorably, the door pressed into her and shoved her back.

With a final push, she stumbled, landing against the arm of the couch. Rain sheeted in and soaked the floor. Lightning cracked in the sky overhead, and she met Alan's deep brown eyes.

Kyla began shaking.

Alan stepped inside the cabin, shut the door behind him, and locked it. Every motion decisive, deliberate.

"Alan." His name slipped like a plea from her lips. A plea to leave her alone, to turn back the clock and undo all the damage he had caused over the past weeks.

He looked her over and smiled softly. A shiver ran down Kyla's back. Alan covered the distance between them and closed his arms around her, his massive body dwarfing hers. She used to love feeling small with him. Now, she felt like a mouse in the embrace of a boa constrictor. He pulled her limp body to his broad chest and kissed the top of her head like he had when they first started dating. Once, she'd ached for him to kiss her more, but now she squirmed in living terror.

Alan had broken into her home and ruined her things. He'd stalked her. Threatened her. Now, he had her arms pinned to her sides, keeping her from wielding the knife still barely clutched in her shaking hand.

Kyla didn't want to be a victim, but believing she could be anything else was difficult.

"What are you doing, Ky?" he asked, holding her closer, tighter. "What are you doing with another man?"

His heart pounded against her cheek, and she closed her eyes. Josh. Where had Josh gone? What had Alan done? She swallowed her fear. "I'm moving on, Alan. You abandoned me. You didn't want me anymore. You broke me."

"You broke up with me, Ky." He tightened his arms around her, and she struggled not to gasp for breath. "You spent more time with your goddamn neighbor than with me. *You* betrayed *me.*"

"What? Dylan?" Kyla opened her eyes and minutely tested his grip. Iron. She could hardly bend her elbows. "Nothing happened with him, I swear."

"I know you were fucking him. A man always knows." His voice rose. She had never seen this side of him.

Kyla swallowed and tilted her head up to look at him. "I wasn't. I haven't."

"No?" He choked out a laugh. His eyes looked wild. "I'll never believe that."

"So you slept with your secretary?" she asked.

He ignored her accusation. "Who the hell is this new guy, then? Don't deny it. I saw him fucking you through the window. I never thought you'd act like such a slut. Were you also fucking him while we were together? Were you *ever* loyal to me?"

Her body went cold. The truth didn't matter to Alan anymore. He'd gone somewhere unreachable. She had to focus all her attention on getting out of his arms.

She blinked the tears out of her eyes and met his furious gaze. "Why did you break into my apartment?"

"You're still mine, Ky. All of you, your things, your place." He grinned lasciviously. "Your panties. Mine." He leaned in close, and she grimaced at the alcohol on his breath. He'd never been a drinker. Had she ever known him at all? As he moved, though, his grip on her loosened.

"You have to leave." She tried to be strong, but her voice trembled.

Alan smiled indulgently. "If I'm leaving, you're coming with me, hon."

Bile rose in her throat.

He bent down to press his dry lips to her mouth. His hands slipped to her waist, and she recognized her chance.

Kyla turned her head away and lifted her free hand to shove at his chest. She darted to the side, heading for the stairs and the phone in the Josh's bedroom.

Alan caught her wrist and crushed it against the solid back of the couch, forcing her to drop the knife. She cried out as white-hot agony raced up her arm. He tutted and circled her slowly, keeping her hand pinned. She made the mistake of meeting his gaze. Something cold and hard observed her from eyes she'd once loved.

"A knife? Ky, you were never going to use that on me." He yanked her in close. "I call the shots here. Don't try anything else like that."

Her shoulder ached from being pulled around by the wrist. If Alan would do this to her, what had he done to Josh? A mixture of fear and adrenaline coursed through her veins. She couldn't run. That left her with one option.

She didn't know much about self-defence, but Dylan had taught her the easiest way to eliminate an unwanted man.

Kyla slammed her elbow into Alan's nose.

Crunch.

"You bitch." He recoiled and cupped his face as blood began to stream. Kyla took the opportunity to bring her knee up between his legs. He bellowed and crumpled, clutching the couch for support.

She had to find Josh.

CHAPTER TWENTY-FIVE

Josh felt his way along the rough side of the cabin. His head pounded like a jackhammer, and he stumbled every few steps, though he couldn't be sure whether he could blame that on the rain-soaked ground or the stars he still saw. His mouth tasted coppery. All he knew was that he had to get back to Kyla.

Josh had made it almost to the door when it slammed open.

"Josh. Oh, my god. Josh." Kyla! Her voice sounded incredibly loud, considering they needed to hide from whoever lurked around the cabin.

"Kyla?" His voice sounded thick and slurred, and it hurt to talk. "Are you okay? Who the hell was that?"

"Alan. He's still inside. We have to move." The panic in her voice chilled him. What had happened? What had Alan done to her?

"Are you okay?" he repeated.

"I don't know." She grabbed Josh's free hand and pulled him away from the cabin door.

He struggled to keep up as Kyla charged through the darkness. As petite as she was, she did an excellent job holding him up.

Josh hissed at the pain when he touched his face. "Your ex got a good punch in."

"So did I." She kept urging him toward Chad's cabin. "Come on. We have to get Dylan."

"I don't think Dylan's in a helpful mood right now..."

"He's a *cop*." Their feet sank deeper into the wet mud with every step they took. "He has to help. I slowed Alan down."

Josh looked over his shoulder just in time to see a shadowy figure limping out of the house toward the woods. He stopped instantly, ignoring Kyla's desperate yanks on his arm.

"He's leaving." Josh leaned against a tree, still unable to see straight. "I'm going back."

"Let him go." She cupped the unhurt side of his face and studied him in the wan moonlight. "You're in no condition to fight him."

Josh closed his eyes. "I'm supposed to be able to protect you."

"I'm okay, Josh."

He winced as he opened his eyes. "I thought you said he was an accountant."

"He is," she said. "I also said he likes the gym. Come on. We need to alert Dylan before Alan gets too far away."

"I'll wait here and keep watch. Will you get Chad or Jer to help me home? I need to lie down."

He didn't want to deal with Dylan in front of an audience, especially not when his head swam like this. Kyla hesitated a moment, then took off running toward Chad's.

All those promises, and he still ended up a shitty boyfriend.

He laughed out loud. Josh had yet to make the boyfriend cut. Rebound, sure. Lover, maybe. He needed to stop getting ahead of himself.

Still.

He looked up at the sound of wet, frantic footsteps. Kyla emerged from the trees with Chad on her heels.

"Hey, buddy. What the hell?" Chad wrapped an arm around Josh's shoulders and eased him off the tree. Josh gratefully shifted his weight.

"Can you help me back to the cabin?" He spat blood. "The fucker left."

"Everybody else is on their way. Jer's tracking down his medical bag, and Dylan's seeing if he can contact the ranger station." Chad began making slow progress back toward the cabin.

"Great. Thanks." Josh shot a wink at Kyla despite how much it hurt. She trailed along behind Chad, drenched and unable to meet his gaze. "Stop looking so guilty. This isn't on you."

"He wouldn't have been here if I wasn't." She reached for his hand and brushed her fingers against his as they traveled the twenty feet back to the cabin. It had felt so much farther in the other direction. "I'm sorry."

"You have nothing to be sorry for, Kyla."

Josh winced his way up the steps to the cabin. Maybe he'd be better on the couch.

"Okay," Chad said as they stepped through the open door. "Wait here, huh? I'll give the place a once-over."

"Be careful," Kyla said.

Chad put up his dukes and grinned before departing. Josh slumped onto the sofa and groaned. His head still pounded, but he couldn't focus on the pain. Instead, he could only think about how the man had snuck up on him, bested him, and threatened his girl.

Kyla smoothed her hand over his hair, and he hissed in pain. "I'm sorry, Josh."

"Stop apologizing," he said. "No one blames you."

"I'm sorry about everything."

He glanced at her as she swiped tears from her cheeks. His arms felt like stone, but he took her hand. "Did Dylan ever tell you about Sky?"

"No, but I think I heard her name when you guys were fighting."

"Dylan was sort of dating her when we were in college. They weren't official or anything, but he really liked her, and he'd taken her out a couple of times. I came over to visit Dylan one night, but he was out."

"And Sky was in?" Kyla asked.

"Yeah. I was eighteen and horny and stupid, and Sky was hot as hell, so when she took off her top, well"—Josh closed his eyes and rested his head against the back of the couch—"you can fill in the rest. Dylan hasn't forgiven me. I've been trying to bribe him with gifts from the bakery since it opened three years ago."

"Okay, but it sounds like she initiated. Dylan dodged a bullet."

Josh opened his eyes and stared at her for a moment. Nobody had ever taken his side. "It takes two," he said haltingly. "I was a very willing participant. I didn't think of my brother's feelings."

Kyla opened her mouth to respond, but Chad stepped back into the room and sat beside them on the sofa. "No one's here."

"Thank god," Josh said.

A knock sounded at the door.

Kyla flinched.

Chad said, "That's probably them."

Kyla stood and walked to the door. She peered through the still-shattered window and visibly exhaled before opening it. Josh cringed when Dylan wrapped his arms around her, whispered in her ear, and kissed her temple. If Josh didn't know any better, he'd say they were dating. As Dylan said, they had a connection. Not just friends, *best* friends. Very close best friends.

Josh barely noticed Tiff and Jer trailing in behind his brother.

"What happened?" Jer walked over to touch Josh's forehead, then his jaw.

"Fuck," Josh hissed.

Jer laughed but kept pressing on his head. "Who's the doctor in the room?"

"You're an EMT."

"Close enough. You lost consciousness?"

Josh could barely listen to his friend. Kyla and Dylan spoke in hushed tones on the other side of the room. He couldn't make out a word.

"Josh. Did you lose consciousness?" Jer repeated.

"I...don't know." He sighed. "Alan definitely broke my face."

"Okay. How do you feel now?"

"Like the Hulk bashed my face in."

Tiff and Chad had begun attempting to fix the window with some tarp, and the sound of ripping tape hit him like an ice pick to the skull.

Josh tried to peer around Jer at Kyla. She and Dylan had stepped off to the side by the stairs. She squatted to scratch Thor's ears while staring up at his brother. She looked calm with him, more relaxed than he'd seen her all day.

He hoped to hell Kyla didn't regret her choice to be with him over Dylan.

CHAPTER TWENTY-SIX

Kyla took a deep breath and met Dylan's gaze. He looked hurt and worried and like he had tried to hide all that under a thick coating of bravado. "We need to talk."

He nodded. "Agreed, but I'd prefer to do that somewhere without a peanut gallery."

She glanced at Josh, splayed across the couch, Jer poking and prodding him. Tiff and Chad had settled in to patch the shattered window. Thor panted and stared back at her from his spot in the kitchen. She couldn't help down here.

Kyla let Dylan lead her up the stairs. They moved in rare silence as if the air around them hung too heavy to push words through. She hated the awkwardness, the tension. At least it chased away the lingering fear of Alan. She had days to file reports and get restraining orders but only a very narrow window to salvage her relationship with her best friend.

Dylan pushed open the door to Josh's bedroom before she could stop him. He inhaled sharply and studied the scene before him. The sheets were nearly off the bed, her bra dangled from the lampshade, and a corner of an open condom wrapper peeked out from underneath a pillow on the floor.

"Dylan—"

Dylan shook his head. "No. I don't want to know. I'm not here for...explanations."

He stayed in the doorway as she pulled the comforter over one half of the bed and sat, then he picked his way to a clear spot in the middle of the room after shutting the door.

Kyla's hands wouldn't stop shaking, so she folded them in her lap. Dylan's gaze never left her.

"I've notified the Park Service," he said suddenly.

Kyla nodded.

"I— We're gonna find Alan. Don't worry." Dylan crossed the room to her with purposeful strides as if he didn't want to look away for fear of what he might see. He sat beside Kyla on the made portion of the bed, so close their shoulders brushed. Kyla wanted to lean away, but she squashed the impulse. He was still her best friend.

She'd had such wonderful ideas of what she'd say to Dylan when she suggested talking. When she looked at him, his familiar face so sad, they all flew out the window.

"So..." She took a deep breath and tried again. "You know I love you, right?"

He snorted, glancing around the room once more. Kyla winced.

"You're my best friend. I don't want to lose you over this, and I don't want Josh to lose you." She took Dylan's hand in hers, and he looked at her hopefully. "So tell me what I can do to fix this."

A smile lit his face, one of the rare slow smiles she loved so much. "Anything?"

"Anything."

"Don't do this." He gestured around the room. "Don't see my brother. I'd like it if you gave me a chance, but I won't demand that of you."

The bottom fell out of Kyla's stomach. She searched Dylan's eyes to see if he could possibly be joking, but she couldn't find the barest hint of humor. Could she give up Josh, the man who had unleashed new parts of her? Could she deny Dylan, her best friend, anything he wanted when he looked at her with those eyes? Her heart thumped unevenly, painfully.

"I love you too, Rosy." Dylan pulled her hand to his lips and spoke against it. "I can fix this, all of this, not just us but Alan, everything. Hell, I'll come up and spend a week at the cabin with you. Whatever you want. Just...not this. I can't take it."

She closed her eyes against the welling tears, knowing everything had just changed. She could never go back to laying on the sofa with Dylan, her head on his chest, while they drank beer and ate junk food. She opened her eyes.

"I asked you," Kyla said haltingly. "After the kiss. I asked you how you felt, and you said it didn't do anything for you."

"I didn't know." Dylan broke eye contact with her for the first time since his request. "Not until you went away."

Kyla hadn't been friends with Dylan for the last three years to not recognize his tells. He'd just held something back from her. She swallowed.

"You didn't know?" she asked. Dylan smoothed his hand down his shorts, another tell. Kyla had never felt so tired or scared, but under that, she had begun to feel pretty damn angry.

"I realized when you were gone, and Alan"—another fidget with the shorts—"disappeared. I realized I couldn't be away from you while you were in danger, job be damned. I wanted to stand by your side."

Kyla pulled her hand slowly out of his. "You said you could fix everything. What do you know about Alan that I don't?"

He blanched, and his throat bobbed as he swallowed. "Alan thinks we were sleeping together."

Kyla shook her head. None of this made any sense. "He accused me of that tonight, but I don't know where he got the idea."

"I do." Dylan exhaled, and his shoulders dropped. "You remember when my shower broke, and you said I could use yours?"

"Yeah, but you never did." Kyla leaned away, unable to tolerate the gentle brush of Dylan's shoulder against hers.

"Maybe you were out with Andrea or working, but I did use it once." Dylan let out another deep breath. "Alan came by right after and confronted me. I didn't even have time to get dressed."

Horror began to dawn on Kyla. "Confronted you about what exactly?"

"He said I was getting in the way of your relationship. Accused me of sleeping with you." Dylan's gaze strayed around the room.

"And you denied that, right?" Kyla had to ask, but she knew what the answer would be.

"Kyla—"

She shook her head and stood. "So, you've known you had feelings for me for months. You ruined my relationship over them. Now you're here when I told you not to come, asking me to give up the first guy I've felt comfortable with since said ruined relationship and to pick you instead?" She could have snarled. She could have thrown up. She began pacing.

"I didn't ruin your relationship on purpose," Dylan said. Kyla whipped a glare at him, and he stopped. "Well, clearly, Alan would've been a bad guy to marry. 'Violent stalker' isn't exactly husband material."

In retrospect, Kyla would pinpoint that as the moment she snapped. Could Alan have gotten in if Dylan hadn't broken the window? Would Alan have ever been that angry if Dylan hadn't lied?

"Dylan Hamilton, you are the lowest scum I've ever had the misfortune of crossing paths with. 'Not exactly husband material.' You didn't lie to my fiancé because you thought he was dangerous. You did it because you thought maybe I would sleep with you someday. God. I really thought—you know what? It doesn't even matter. Josh told me about Sky today, and I should have realized then and there that you're nothing more than a selfish hypocrite."

Dylan stood, temper rising. Kyla should have felt small in the face of such a towering wall of police-trained fury, but it seemed like nothing could quell her right then.

"I'm going to forgive that." Dylan's voice sounded icy, a voice she'd never heard before. "Because I don't think you know what you're talking about. Otherwise, you wouldn't be throwing in my face the fact my brother fucked my girlfriend."

Kyla began laughing, near hysterical. "Sky fucked your brother. Not exactly 'girlfriend material.' And you've been raking him over the coals for it for nearly a decade! Call me in seven years, then we'll see how I feel about you destroying my relationship."

"I'm going to leave now," Dylan said through gritted teeth. "Before either of us say anything we're really going to regret."

He turned and stormed out of the room, slamming the door behind him. Silence fell. All the anger drained from Kyla's body, and she collapsed on the bed, curling into a small ball. Exhaustion seeped into her bones. She couldn't remember the last time she'd felt so tired, but how could she sleep? Alan had hunted her like an animal and attacked her in a place she felt safe. She'd basically slept for years beside a monster without ever suspecting. Moreover, after Dylan's confession, how could she ever trust her judgment again?

A soft knock sounded on the door, and Josh peeked his

bandaged head into the room. His brow wrinkled when he saw her, and she immediately sat up.

"Are you all right?" He stepped in and closed the door behind him.

"You're the one with the head wound." Kyla smiled humorlessly. "I should be asking you."

He smiled. "Jer's a paramedic. He says I ought to see my doctor when I get home to be safe, but I should be okay with a little rest."

Kyla stood abruptly. "Well, lie down then."

Josh obeyed with an indulgent smile, and she tucked him in. Tears welled in her eyes, but she ignored them and kissed his forehead.

"Kyla. Come to bed with me." Josh patted the other side of his mattress, the bed they'd shared that afternoon. "They all left. Chad and Tiff finished patching the window, so we can deal with everything tomorrow, or hell, later today, but for now, it's just us, okay?"

Kyla perched on the edge of the bed next to him, and he wound his arms around her waist. She couldn't be trusted to make safe choices, to bring safe people into her life, but Josh clung to her like a life raft. She swallowed back a sob.

"Tiff said she had an idea how Alan might be tracking you, something about GPS. She's the big IT girl, so I could barely follow, but she said she could fix it. Now will you sleep?"

Clarity dawned on Kyla. She wasn't safe. She could blame it on other people for as long as she liked, but the common denominator would always be her. She lifted her chin and met Josh's eyes.

"Don't." Josh's voice sounded nearly frantic. "Whatever you're about to say, please don't. I've never felt like this before, and I don't think you have either. Don't ruin it because my brother said something stupid. We could be amazing if you just give us a chance.”

She blinked, and tears fell. “We were amazing, Josh, but that's over now.”

CHAPTER TWENTY-SEVEN

Josh struggled upright in bed, his head swimming with every move. "Why?"

Kyla's chest heaved, and high, red spots appeared on her cheeks. Josh wanted to reach out and smooth her wrinkled brow, but he was too scared she'd flinch, which would break his heart.

"Kyla, why?"

Kyla crossed her arms over her chest and looked at him warily. "I don't think you want to hear my reasons."

Josh scrubbed a hand over his face. The room swam a little, and he leaned back against the headboard for support. What he wouldn't give for a working brain right now.

"I need something." Josh laid his hand, palm up, on the comforter. She could take it if she wanted to. "I can't just let you go." Not when he'd spent the last three days feeling things he'd never previously felt.

Kyla stared at his hand for a moment. "It's just not fair."

Josh blinked. "Not fair? I've been over this a dozen times in my head, and I can't come up with a reason not to be with you. Dylan will get over this. Tasha's a thing of the past. We can file a restraining order against Alan or something. Kyla, I—"

"Not fair to me, Josh."

Her words silenced him. He didn't even know what he'd been about to say. Something ridiculous. Words that shouldn't be thrown around in the first few days of knowing someone. He'd started getting ahead of himself again.

He let out a heavy breath.

Kyla stood and stepped well out of arms' reach. He wished he could trust his body to support him if he reached forward and pulled her back.

"You're fun." She smiled softly. "A lot of fun. And I've had a lot of fun with you. But to see someone long-term, I need more than that. I need someone steady, someone responsible. Someone I can count on."

Josh took that like a second blow to the head. Someone she could count on. She might as well have said Dylan would make a better husband than he ever could.

Husband?

He needed to go to sleep.

"Okay." The word tasted like dirt in his mouth. She took a tentative step forward but seemed to stop herself.

"I'm sorry. You're a really good guy. I mean that. I just..." Kyla looked around the room and bit her lip. "I just don't think we're right for each other."

"Yeah, I get it." His voice sounded toneless and strange. The world around him took on a grayish tone.

"I think you could make someone really, really happy," she said.

Josh sighed. "Just say you got what you wanted from me and go."

Kyla froze. "What I wanted?"

He dropped his head back and closed his eyes. "I was, what,

rebound sex? A confidence booster? It's life. I get it. I just wish you hadn't pretended this was anything more than that."

A long, awful silence followed. His head jackhammered. He felt tired and sore and stupid.

"Josh, I—" Kyla sighed. "I'm sorry."

The door to his bedroom opened, then closed.

CHAPTER TWENTY-EIGHT

The hallway clock chimed four in the morning. The next day. A continuation of the longest day of Kyla's life.

She just wanted to go home.

A thump and a groan came from behind the closed bedroom door. She squared her shoulders and kept walking.

If Kyla could just get to her car, she would be okay. If she could just get out, forget this place, erase everything that had happened in the last few days, she might be able to survive the way Josh had looked at her as she left.

Kyla fled down the stairs as fast as she could manage. The less she remembered about the cabin, the better. Once she reached the living room, she packed her scattered clothes into her bag, then grabbed her camera case from the bag they'd hiked with. Most of her things were still in the bedroom, but she could get them another time. Or buy new things.

She couldn't even ask Dylan to get them.

The rain pounded outside, and her only jacket hung in the closet of the room where she'd left Josh. The stairs creaked behind her. Josh leaned on the wall, squinting against the light. She'd caused that pain, too.

"Don't leave. Not right now. It's late, or early, and you haven't slept," he said. He sounded more tired than sad now.

"I can't stay, Josh. Not when..." She couldn't say the words. She couldn't even think them. She spotted Josh's hoodie and grabbed it as she moved toward the door.

"Kyla."

She turned. Josh pushed himself out from the wall, and she could have sworn she saw tears in his eyes.

"Goodbye." She opened the door and stepped into the pouring rain.

She didn't start crying until she had pulled out of the driveway, taken three wrong turns in the dark, and finally made it out to the main road. The storm billowed around her as she raced back to the lonely monotony of her life in Missoula. Home wouldn't be the same now, though. Between Alan and Dylan, how could she relax?

Dammit.

She had no one to go to and nowhere to go. The cabin lay behind her, and home couldn't be trusted. Maybe she could find a roadside motel? Somewhere no one could find her. Wait, hadn't Josh said something about Alan using a tracker? Fuck.

Kyla flipped the wipers to the highest speed and peered through the bleary windshield at the road ahead. The pounding rain roiled on the asphalt like hot butter in a pan. Naturally, she was the only driver on this cliffside mountain road, coming or going. Everyone else stayed tucked safe and dry in their cabins, fires warming their toes.

She scrubbed her tearstained cheeks. She had never felt more humiliated, more homesick, more alone. She needed Dylan's comforting arms, but they wouldn't feel the same. She craved Josh's lips against hers, but she couldn't handle the consequences. She needed one of Andrea's killer margaritas, with extra lime and twice the tequila, but she lay beyond a three-hour drive.

Kyla found herself well and truly alone.

Her stomach vibrated. This time it wasn't nerves or sheer, guttural sadness. She slid her hand into the pocket of Josh's hoodie and met cool metal and glass. She'd stolen his cell phone. Shit.

She didn't want to answer. She didn't want to hear whatever Josh had to say or whatever Dylan had to say to Josh. Or, worst of all, anything Tasha had on her mind.

A sob slipped from her lips at the thought of Josh's beautiful face. The face she would never wake to. The breath-stealing blue eyes she would never gaze into again. The hungry lips she would crave for the rest of her days.

She couldn't talk to him. If she heard his warm, deep voice, she would turn around. Kyla knew she wouldn't be strong enough to walk away twice. She'd made mistakes with her lousy judgment of men more than once, and she couldn't risk him being another bad judgment call.

Also, now she knew Alan was violent, she couldn't risk Josh's safety.

The vibrations stopped, then restarted.

"Go away," she said through clenched teeth.

Lightning cracked through the sky, illuminating what would have been a beautiful cliffside view under normal circumstances. God, she hadn't even made it out of the park yet.

Another set of vibrations. "Dammit, Josh. Leave me alone."

The vibrations began again. This guy did not give up. "Okay. If it rings one more time—"

A quiet moment passed, and Kyla felt new tears fall down her cheeks. Then, the phone started vibrating once more.

With a deep exhale, Kyla pulled the phone out of Josh's pocket. She smiled at the goofy photo of a college-age Dylan looking back at her from the screen. The other Hamilton brother who had broken her heart.

She picked up the call.

"Hey." She tried to sound normal—as if she hadn't just been sobbing.

"Rosy? Where are you?" Dylan sounded tense, serious. Straight-up cop mode. She could barely make out his voice through the pelting rain.

"I'm on the road. Going home. Or not. I don't know. I just left."

"Okay. Clearly, I missed something because it's the middle of the night in a fucking thunderstorm. Jesus, Kyla." He sighed. "Pull over."

"I don't care."

"You don't care? If you crash that car, I'm going to kill you. It's not safe."

"Oh, great, now I have two people who want to kill me." She swatted a fresh fall of tears. "I'm a good driver, anyway. I'm fine."

"Fuck. Kyla. Just pull over. I'll be right there." She heard a tinny rattle of keys through the phone. "Where are you?"

"Dylan—"

"Please tell me where you are."

He sounded so comforting, so much like he used to, that her eyes stung. She blinked rapidly, struggling to see the road. "I've ruined everything."

"Calm down, Kyla. We'll get this sorted out. You just need to tell me where you are."

"Dylan, I've ruined everything."

"I'm sitting in my truck. Just point me in a direction."

"I broke up with Josh. You two should patch things up. He's more than done his time, Dill. I'll move or something. Have a good life." Kyla hung up the phone and wiped her eyes. She had to focus on driving. If she could get to Andrea's, maybe everything would be okay.

She placed the phone in the cupholder, where it immediately began vibrating with another call from Dylan. She gripped the wheel with both hands and steadfastly ignored it. She just had to start her whole life over. Alone. No big deal. She swiped away an additional round of tears.

Another set of headlights pulled onto the road behind her. Even just seeing somebody else was a comfort. Some other soul had chosen to brave the night with her.

The driver picked up speed and were soon mere feet from the back of her car. She squinted against the intensity of the headlights in her rear-view mirror. Of course, she had to share the road with a high-beam asshole. That certainly wouldn't make the drive any easier.

She huffed a sigh, half-pleased to let irritation overtake her sadness for a moment.

The driver laid on their horn, and she checked her speedometer. During the call with Dylan, she'd let it creep up past forty, far faster than she'd normally drive in a storm like this. Whoever wanted her to go even faster could wait or swerve into the empty second lane if they were that antsy. Kyla felt briefly grateful she was driving on the opposite side as the cliff, though the dense thicket of trees and brush on her side didn't look particularly welcoming.

The car behind her drew closer, so close she almost thought they'd make contact, and she realized with a swoop of her stomach that it was black.

Like Alan's.

She shook her head. Black four-doors weren't exactly rare, and the jump in violence between punching Josh in the head and running her off the road seemed insurmountable. Alan wouldn't do something like that.

The rain had picked up substantially. The windshield wipers, even at their fastest setting, struggled to hold back the tide. Kyla leaned forward in her seat and squinted into the blur. The clouds hung heavy and low overhead. She should pull over. These were not safe driving conditions, but between the car behind her and her stubbornness, she couldn't make herself stop.

The phone began vibrating with another call, and she ignored it. Dylan wouldn't change her mind, not now. The vibrations stopped, then began again. She glanced down in time to see a number scrolling across the screen. Kyla recognized it instantly.

Alan.

Goose bumps pebbled her skin. How had he gotten Josh's number? Why would Alan call her now? Confused about whether she should answer, she did nothing. The phone stopped vibrating, then immediately started again. Same number. She didn't know what Alan would do if she refused him again. With shaking hands, Kyla picked up and answered the phone.

"H-hello?" She tucked the phone between her chin and shoulder so she could hold onto the steering wheel.

"Hello, Kyla." Alan's voice sounded sinister against the pounding rain. Kyla shivered. "I'm glad I found you. We didn't get to finish our conversation earlier."

That same panic from before began to lock down her limbs. Her grip on the steering wheel became iron. "I suppose not."

"No, you ended things quite rudely. I believe you broke my nose. And now I've had to come out in this storm." Another crack of lightning split the sky, drawing attention to the road where it grew even narrower. The black car behind her, Alan's car, edged slightly closer. "I think I'd like an apology before I take you back."

"I'm sorry I broke your nose." The apology spilled from her lips, rote and defensive. She wished she could bite it back. She'd break Alan's nose a dozen more times if she had the chance. A deep, simmering anger kindled in her chest.

Alan hummed thoughtfully. "That's not quite enough. I want an apology for everything. Then, we can go back to planning your dream wedding, just the way you liked it."

"Everything?" Another bolt of lightning cracked through the sky. She spotted a sharp curve in the road ahead, overlooking yet another beautiful cliffside vista.

"Everything. Hitting me. Dumping me. Sleeping with that cop in the first place. *Everything.*" Alan growled the last word, a bit of that animal rage she'd seen earlier seeping through his conversational façade.

Kyla was angry. And tired. And motherfucking done. She'd spent all day being pushed around and humiliated. Tasha. Alan. Even Dylan and Josh had played their parts.

"No," she said quietly.

"What?" Alan swerved his car closer and back again, an obvious threat. She sped up a little more to get out of his range, but he only matched her. She was trapped. Her only options were to tuck her tail between her legs and give up or fight back.

Kyla inhaled deeply. "No."

"You little bitch. You slut. You whore. I deserve an apology for what you put me through—"

"I didn't put you through anything." The anger in her chest burned bright. She suddenly became glad Alan had called because she needed him to hear this. "Not a single thing! Dylan *lied,* and you were too irrational and jealous to see through it. Even before that, you were controlling and dismissive and never listened when I asked you for anything. You were a bad boyfriend, and you know what, Alan?" She breathed hard and thought of Josh and the way he smiled when she asked about his tattoo. "I deserve better."

The car juddered forward with an awful crunch, audible even over the thunder and rain, and Kyla slammed into her steering wheel. Her vision went red, and her head swam. Blearily, she remembered the turn ahead and stomped on her brakes.

Another, heavier weight pounded against the back of her car. Her head slammed forward. The sound of metal on metal seemed to go on forever. Her car hydroplaned, spinning almost gracefully on the slick asphalt. Her world spun with it, and everything went dark.

* * *

WHEN SHE BLINKED HER EYES OPEN AGAIN, SHE DANGLED SIDEWAYS AT the bottom of a marshy trench, held in place only by her seatbelt, and her airbag had slowly begun to deflate. She slowly checked herself over for injuries. All her limbs moved with relative ease, albeit with extreme soreness. A cut on her head seemed to have produced the blood all over the airbag, and it hurt like hell to breathe, but otherwise she seemed mostly fine.

In a haze of pain, she switched the car off, pocketed the keys, and kicked against the door with all her might. She could not get stuck down here. She could not end her night like that. Her ribs screamed at her, but finally, the door flew open. She slung her camera bag over her shoulder, scrambled shakily out, and beheld the scene in front of her.

Her pink Beetle lay on its side, halfway submerged in muck. White tendrils of smoke swirled into the black sky from the rear engine, but it seemed like the relentless sheet of rain kept anything from catching fire. She opened the trunk, though she had no idea what to look for. Soaked to the bone, she blankly beheld the giant puzzle of dirty metal, hoses, steam, and wires.

Giving up on the engine, she stood still, trying her hardest to listen over the sound of the torrential downpour. Nothing. Maybe Alan had driven away after knocking her into the ditch? God, she hoped so. She only knew two self-defence tricks, and she'd already used them.

After a few minutes, and ignoring the pain in her ribs, she pulled herself out of the muddy ditch using tufts of wildflowers and deep-rooted grasses, then used the rest of her strength to hoist herself onto a large, flat rock close to the top of the ditch. Her body ached, and she would've given anything at that moment to be able to curl up and sleep.

There were no signs of Alan, but she couldn't see more than a foot in front of her face with the rain bouncing off the asphalt. She needed a phone, and she'd forgotten to look for it in the car. Dammit. She couldn't go back down there.

Suddenly, on the horizon, she spotted a set of headlights.

It couldn't be Alan because the direction was wrong, but still, she prayed it wasn't him. She stumbled a little closer to the top of the ditch and cautiously waved her arms, careful of her damaged ribs.

The car drove right by, splashing her in its wake.

She could have cried, but before she had a chance to give in to fear, pain, and fatigue, a second pair of headlights shone through the blinding rain.

This set, thank god, pulled over.

Kyla held her hand above her eyes, trying to shield them from the headlights and rain so she could see her champion. However, from the shiver that ran through her body as his silhouette approached, a shiver that had nothing to do with the rain, she knew exactly who had found her.

CHAPTER TWENTY-NINE

Josh's heart thudded against his ribs. The barrier between the cliff and the road was now a pile of twisted metal, but the small figure who stood at the top of a ditch, her bug sitting sideways at the bottom, mainly looked unharmed. Somebody else must've wrecked the barrier. His heart finally slowed.

"What the hell, Kyla?" Josh peered through the heavy downpour at her. Her clothes were soaked, and she shivered violently.

Kyla crossed her arms. "Excuse me?"

The visibility in this weather had gone from bad to nothing in minutes, and she'd been driving on slick roads she didn't know. She should have pulled over. Josh found himself fighting the unexpected urge to tell her that, but Kyla wasn't the type to enjoy a lecture under the best of circumstances.

"Come here." Josh dug his hiking boots deep into the wet grass and stepped closer to check her for injuries. She stepped away.

That hurt.

"Please, let me—"

"No. I don't... I don't want you to touch me." Pain flashed

across her beautiful features. Kyla looked small as she stood there. So lost, so helpless, so alone. The trees towered behind her against a pitch-black sky, and he had to shout over the storm to be heard.

"I need to make sure you're all right." He stepped forward again, and this time, with a steep ditch behind her, she stayed put. "You're bleeding." Josh ran his fingers over the wound on her forehead, just above her left eyebrow.

"I'll live. I can fix this on my own."

Josh shut his eyes for a second. A small, bitter part of him wanted to let her try getting out of this storm by herself. She didn't seem to have changed her mind since they last talked. She didn't want him here, but he'd leaped into his car when Dylan called him, concussion notwithstanding.

"Come back to the cabin with me." His voice sounded desperate. He wanted to fix this. He wanted to say whatever he needed to say, do whatever he needed to do, to be the man she wanted.

He'd only had her for a few days. They'd been beautiful, but he wanted more. He'd gotten greedy.

"No." She shook her head, then winced. "I'm going home. To Missoula."

Josh crossed his arms now. "Not in that car, you're not."

She huffed. "Obviously." She ran her hands over her soaked hair, then, as if the idea had just dawned on her, pulled up the hood of the sweatshirt. "I'll walk. Or I'll hitchhike."

"Like hell you will. Stop being so damn stubborn and come home with me."

A *boom* louder than he could have previously imagined echoed off the asphalt. Heat blossomed against his back, the ground shook, and the world turned blindingly orange.

Josh stumbled forward, remembered the ditch, grabbed Kyla, and rolled them sideways to avoid falling.

His head spun viciously, but after a moment, the heat and noise ceased. The orange light remained, though dimmer and flickering gently.

Kyla lay on top of him, face twisted in pain. He'd caged her in place, but he let go, and she got unsteadily to her feet. He followed, and together, they peered over the edge of the cliff where the explosion had come from. Half-suspended on a rock shelf a few hundred feet down sat the wreck of a burning car that sent up plumes of smoke and that orange light.

Kyla lifted a shaking hand to her mouth. "Your phone is in the car."

"What?" He had no idea what she was going on about. How had his phone gotten in the burning car?

She turned to face him, the fire reflecting in her eyes. "My car. Get it. We have to call 911!"

Josh started sprinting before he'd even fully processed leaving an injured woman at the scene of a wreck. Nausea roiled in his stomach, threatening to halt his progress, but he spat and kept moving. He slid down the bank of the ditch and hopped in the still-open door of the Beetle. After a few moments of scrabbling in the muck that had begun seeping into the downward-facing side of the car, he got his phone.

The climb back up the hill took a toll. He could see the route Kyla used, but every time he leaned back, the world threatened to turn upside down. By the time he'd made it back to her side, Kyla had lowered herself to the ground directly in front of the broken barrier.

He sat next to her and offered the device. She took it and dialed with shaking hands.

"There's been an accident. Somebody is really hurt. We're..." She looked at him. God, she didn't even know what road she was on. He took the phone back.

"We're on Going-to-the-Sun Road, a little past the Jackson Glacier Overlook. Please come quickly."

"All right, we're dispatching someone to your location." A clipped, professional voice crackled over the line. Josh thanked them and hung up the phone.

Kyla looked at him, face blotchy. She seemed exhausted. He got to his feet, crouched, scooped her up bridal style, and started for his Jeep. He didn't even consider his dizziness until she was in his arms, but she seemed less stable than he was, and he couldn't leave her out here, no matter what else happened.

Josh's head swam as he moved, but one thing felt perfectly clear: he could get used to saving Kyla. Except she didn't seem to want him to save her. Though apparently stunned for a few seconds when he scooped her up, she wasn't anymore.

"Put me down!"

"Stop squirming." Josh held her tighter to his chest, careful not to drop his feisty but precious cargo.

"We have to wait for the ambulance." Her voice was barely audible over the next clap of thunder.

"We can wait in the car."

When he sat her, wet and shivering, on the passenger seat of his Jeep, she belted him with her fists, and as he drew the seatbelt across her chest, she slapped at his hands. So wildly independent. So opinionated and strong-willed.

He had started falling in love with this girl.

Josh found himself neither surprised nor bothered by the thought as he ran to the driver's side. He wanted to be in love with her. Though he couldn't shake the wave of shame and hurt that had overcome him when she'd said he was just fun, Kyla was worth the fight to keep her—and he would fight. Whether Dylan accepted that or not didn't matter. Josh couldn't let her go.

He hopped in the Jeep and looked at her. She stared at the plume of smoke beyond the cliff's ridge.

"Kyla. *Kyla.*"

Finally, she looked at him. He barely resisted the urge to cup her cheek.

"Tell me what happened."

"I... I don't want to." She bit her lip, and tears shimmered in her eyes.

"Why not?" Josh turned on the car and dialed up the heat.

"You won't look at me again. Not anymore because I—" She swallowed hard, and tears slid down her face.

"What, Kyla? What did you do?"

She shook her head and turned her face away. Josh gave in to his need and slid his hand over her cheek, turning her to face him. "No matter what you did or think you did, I will always want to look at you."

"Even if I killed Alan?"

At that, she began to shake and cry uncontrollably. Josh ached to draw her into his arms, but he settled for placing a hand on her shoulder while he tried to figure out what she meant.

The smoking wreck had looked like a small car, maybe dark in color. Alan's car. He must have followed her when she left.

Josh seriously doubted she'd killed Alan, at least intentionally. With these road conditions, somebody could go off the edge without doing something stupid, and he'd bet money Alan had done something quite stupid.

Josh's jaw throbbed in agreement.

So, he waited and let her cry. Eventually, her tears tapered, and as an emergency siren whined in the distance, she looked up at him with glittering green eyes. Beautiful eyes.

"The ambulance is almost here. Tell me what happened."

Kyla sniffled. "He pulled up behind me. He must've still

been tracking me. I thought he was just an asshole on the road, but then, he called me on your phone. He asked me to apologize. For hitting him. For sleeping with Dylan, which I didn't even do. And"—she took a breath and seemed to gather herself—"I got mad. I was fed up with things happening to me that I had no control over, and I told him *no*. So he rammed his car into the back of mine."

"He hit you?" Impotent rage bubbled up in Josh. What would lead someone to be so reckless? Then, he remembered Alan had lost Kyla. Maybe his choices made a little more sense.

Kyla nodded. "I didn't know what to do, so I braked and spun off into that little ditch, and he... He..."

She dissolved into tears again. Red-and-white flashing lights rounded the corner, then two ambulances and a firetruck pulled to a stop in front of the Jeep.

Josh turned her to face him once more. He smiled. He could smile at her forever. He realized he hadn't just started falling in love with her—he'd gone full head-over-heels.

"Kyla?"

She wiped away a tear. "Yeah?"

"I'm still looking at you."

CHAPTER THIRTY

KYLA STRUGGLED TO SORT THROUGH HER JUMBLED THOUGHTS, BUT breathing was a challenge, let alone deciphering her feelings.

Alan, the man she had once loved, lay trapped in a mess of steel and flames at the bottom of a mountain. He had stalked her, scared her, and tried to force her into the same fate, but she still couldn't picture the world without him in it.

Josh sat in the car next to her, whole and hale. He looked so earnest, but a part of her wondered if he would have come to find her if Dylan hadn't called him.

Amid the throbbing aches that made up her body, Kyla scraped her fingers through her hair and came back with a handful of mud. She desperately wanted to take a long bath and face everything else tomorrow, but the cacophony of sirens outside suggested she'd get no such thing.

The passenger door of Josh's Jeep opened, and Kyla flinched before reminding herself she didn't have to worry about Alan. Instead of the paramedic she expected to see, Dylan stood there.

Before she could speak, he folded her up in his big, strong arms and kissed the top of her head. He held her close, too close considering the lancing pain in her ribcage, but she couldn't find the heart to push him off.

"I'm so sorry, Rosy," he mumbled into her hair.

She wanted to be righteous and angry, but she just felt hurt. Dylan hadn't meant to cause any of this. She knew that. But knowing it didn't make it any easier to forgive as the fire crackled away behind him.

"I know." They needed to talk, but she couldn't. Not now. Not when she was barely holding it together.

Relief flooded her when a burly paramedic got Dylan's attention, and not just from the lessened ache in her chest.

"Does anyone need medical attention?" he asked.

"She does," Josh and Dylan answered in unison. The brothers exchanged a glance, and she looked away.

"My car went off the road," she said as the man pressed cotton to her bleeding forehead.

"Are you in pain anywhere else?"

She nodded and set her hand on her lower right ribs. Even that light touch set off a new string of aches. "Something hurts here."

The man stepped back to make room for his partner with the stretcher. "I'd like to take you in. Make sure there isn't anything worse going on than bruised ribs."

"Northern Rockies Medical Center?" Josh asked.

"Yes, sir."

The paramedic helped her onto the stretcher. Dylan and Josh followed alongside her in the rain.

Kyla had never been inside an ambulance before. She'd never so much as had a concussion. Nerves threatened to overwhelm her, but the paramedics moved her so seamlessly that she hardly noticed getting inside.

Both Hamilton brothers peered through the open back

doors, waiting for an invitation. Her stomach flipped, and she almost forgot about the pain.

"Riding alone?" the burly paramedic asked.

She nodded, and another paramedic closed the doors. Josh and Dylan, framed in each of the small windows, bore identical expressions of disappointment.

Kyla closed her eyes.

The paramedic slipped an oxygen mask over her face, and she tried to relax while he poked and prodded at her ribs. When he hit the sorest point, she barely choked back a scream. He nodded tersely.

"Is there anyone we can call for you?" he asked.

"No." The word caught in her throat. She thought of Alan, dying alone on a mountainside, and tears began to flow down her face anew.

"Try to take deep breaths, okay?" The paramedic offered a sympathetic smile. "I'm Andrew, by the way. And I understand how scary a car accident can be. They're especially dangerous on these narrow mountain roads."

"Alan"—she swallowed back the pain and betrayal—"my former fiancé went over the side. He couldn't have..."

"Survived? I don't know, but it doesn't seem likely. I've seen too many people go off those cliffs. I know search-and-rescue will confirm, though. I'm sorry for your loss if not."

She nodded. "He tried to take me over with him."

Andrew grimaced very slightly, then checked a machine over her head. "But you're going to be okay. I just need you to try and stay calm. I know you're rattled, but your blood pressure is extremely elevated."

Kyla took a slow breath and tried to steady herself. She couldn't remember the last time she'd been in this much pain. "I'm really tired."

"I know. But I need you to stay awake until we get to the

hospital." Andrew's fingers were cool as he dressed her forehead.

Her eyes fluttered shut anyway. She envisioned Dylan and Josh, looking into the ambulance at her. She loved them both, but each of them had hurt her.

Love, it seemed, didn't come without pain.

CHAPTER THIRTY-ONE

Josh tipped his head back to the sky. Driving rain pelted his face, and it felt so much colder than it had when he'd left the Jeep with Kyla earlier. "Fuck."

"You can say that again," Dylan said. He stared after Kyla's ambulance, though it had long since disappeared around a turn.

Josh made up his mind. "I'm going to the hospital."

Dylan choked on a laugh. "She doesn't want us there. She more than made that clear."

"I don't care. She's going to need a ride." Josh stalked to his Jeep, and Dylan trailed behind. "She can ignore me, or yell at me, or whatever she wants, but I'm not leaving her stranded hours from home. Not after the day she's had."

Dylan nodded. "Okay, then I'm coming with you. Nobody's going out in this storm, so my car will be fine."

Josh sighed. He recognized the set of Dylan's jaw. No use arguing.

This was going to be a long-ass night.

"It's okay to leave the scene?" Josh asked Dylan as they got into the car. Small talk seemed safe enough.

"Yeah. We weren't involved. I left my number with someone, and I'm fairly certain the police will follow Kyla to the hospital for her side of the story."

"Good, good." Josh nodded. He rolled his shoulders. Did he ask about the weather next? He felt like such a moron. He used to be able to talk to Dylan for hours.

Dylan folded his arms. "Listen—"

"I don't want to fight right now," Josh said.

"I just said listen," Dylan snapped. He closed his eyes and took a deep breath. When he opened them again, he looked steadier. "You don't have to say anything."

Josh nodded. He'd be fine as long as Dylan didn't start yelling.

"Rosy let me have it last night." Josh glanced at his brother. Dylan stared out the window.

"Yeah?"

Dylan sighed. "She said a lot of things, most of them probably true. That I'm scum and so on."

"She probably didn't mean that." Josh would be lying if he said he wasn't a little pleased to hear he wasn't the only one on the receiving end of Kyla's anger, but even with everything his brother had done, he didn't deserve to be called scum.

"No, no. She's right. I've been too tough on you. Sky wasn't exactly my true love. We shouldn't still be talking about her this many years later." He groaned. "And I'm sorry for being the asshole who keeps bringing it up."

Josh looked back at him, eyes wide. "What was that?"

Dylan crossed his arms. "Just accept the apology, asshole."

A wave of relief flooded Josh, and he laughed with the rush of it. He wished they weren't racing to a hospital so he could hug his brother for the first time in years. Maybe they could start watching baseball together again. None of his friends liked it, and no one hollered at the ump quite like Dylan.

"I'm sorry, Dylan. I accept. And for the record. I should never have gone all the way with Sky. I was young and stupid and selfish." Josh tried to look contrite, but he couldn't quite keep the grin off his face.

"You were, but I can't hold that over you for your whole life." Dylan sighed heavily, and Josh realized his brother didn't seem quite so thrilled.

"So...are we good?" he asked.

A long silence fell. The grin slipped off Josh's face.

"Is it Kyla?" Out of the corner of his eye, Josh watched Dylan turn to him and just look. His heart thumped unevenly.

"I know this sucks, but... I kinda miss having a brother."

Dylan looked away again.

Josh sighed. Well, it had been a good two minutes. He switched on the radio and resigned himself to returning home with nothing but his bakery to keep him company.

They'd traveled nearly another twenty minutes before Dylan finally spoke up.

"Me, too. Just...not yet."

Josh nodded. A small, stupid burst of hope welled up in him. Not yet might mean he only had a snowball's chance in hell, but that was better than what he'd started the week with. He could wait. He knew how to do that well enough.

They drove the rest of the way to the hospital in relative silence, Dylan simply telling him where to turn, and when to pass someone.

When they arrived at the hospital, Dylan took off for a walk in the thankfully lessening rain. He clearly needed a little space. Josh rushed inside and up to the desk just as the burly paramedic from the scene pushed Kyla's stretcher through the emergency doors.

"Oh, that's— I'm here to see—" He ignored the protests of

the admittance staff and ran behind the desk to follow along beside Kyla.

Kyla offered him a shy smile and reached for his hand. The protests behind him stopped when Kyla raised her other hand. "He can stay." Her voice cracked as she spoke. She had an oxygen mask, a bandage on her head, and an industrial-strength icepack on her chest.

His heart ached. He didn't want to be the asshole who broke the rules, but timing seemed crucial with Kyla, and he couldn't let things fester.

Josh kept pace with the stretcher until they reached a small, private room.

The doctor checked her over, and Josh stayed out of the way. Kyla winced every time they prodded at her ribs, and Josh wished he could tell the doctor to stop hurting her. She'd broken one rib and bruised the rest on that side, but it didn't seem likely to puncture anything important. Beyond a few stitches in her head, she got a clean bill of health.

When the room finally cleared, Josh sat on the edge of her bed and reached for her hand. "Hey."

"Hey, you." She accepted his hand and studied the back of it.

"How do you feel?" He could've smacked himself. What was it about this girl that made him act like such an idiot?

Luckily, she smiled. "Like I got hit by a car."

"I know the feeling." He rubbed his jaw. Maybe he should check into the hospital while he was here.

Kyla's face fell. "Alan. Is he..."

Josh brought her hand to his lips and kissed the back of it. He hated to tell her, to confirm her fears. "I think so."

She paled. Her hand trembled slightly in his. "Okay. Okay. That's fine. Okay."

Tears fell down Kyla's face, and Josh reached forward to

swipe them away. Kyla leaned into his touch. Another good sign.

"Do you want to hear the stupidest part?" she mumbled.

Josh nodded.

"I can't stop thinking about you and Dylan. I'm a murderer, and I'm worrying about my romantic drama." She choked out a laugh.

"You're not a murderer," Josh replied instantly. "The cops at the scene kept calling it an accident. Because it was. I'm happy to be a sounding board if you need one."

Kyla smiled, but she looked bitter. Josh just wanted to see her happy again.

"I feel so guilty that he hit you outside the cabin, Josh. That I brought all this trouble with me." She sighed. "It's suffocating."

"No, Kyla. What he did, that's not—"

Her eyes flashed. "Let me finish."

"I'm sorry." He nodded. "Keep going."

"And my heart aches over Dylan. I'm praying I didn't lead him on and make him think I wanted more. I feel horrible that I didn't tell you that Dylan kissed me before you and I had sex. I'm so angry with Dylan for holding your mistake with Sky against you for so long and for making this, us, about him."

Josh hoped his smile was reassuring. "Dylan and I rode up here together."

Her eyes widened. "Really?"

"Mm. He's outside. He's worried about you, too."

She crushed her bottom lip between her teeth. "I said horrible things to him."

"Whatever you said seemed to knock some sense into him." Josh couldn't help but smile as he thought about Dylan and his conversation. "We're working it out."

She pulled their hands to her heart. "Really?" She tried to

laugh, but it turned into a wince. "I'm so excited for you. For both of you."

"Me, too." He tried to sound enthusiastic, but he felt more worried than excited. Josh didn't want Kyla to push him away to save his relationship with his brother.

Kyla looked him over. "What aren't you telling me?"

She could very nearly read his mind already. Josh took a deep breath, but before he could say anything, she frowned.

"He's not okay with us, is he?"

He exhaled in a gust. "Fuck, Kyla. I'm so sorry. For everything. I need to say that I didn't mean anything I said when you were leaving. It was stupid. I was hurt, and I wanted you to hurt. But I have to ask. Did you?"

Her eyebrows furrowed. "Did I?"

"Mean it. That I was just...fun." Josh's stomach churned. He'd respect whatever she said, but god, he hoped she'd been lying.

"I needed you not to follow me," she said weakly. "I never should have said it."

Josh's shoulders slumped with relief. He wished he could be certain Kyla would accept a kiss from him. "I talked to Dylan, and I don't think you can have both of us. At least, not right now. I thought the last thing I wanted was to piss him off, but the last thing I want is to lose you."

She nodded, and his heart fell. If she couldn't have both of them, maybe it was better to have neither. Maybe he didn't have her heart the way she had his.

Kyla opened her mouth to speak, and a doctor entered the room.

CHAPTER THIRTY-TWO

The doctor moved Kyla to a private room where she'd wait out the remaining hours she had to spend in this hospital. Apparently, even with just one fractured rib, she had to be monitored for "complications." Both Hamilton brothers had taken it upon themselves to hover. She wanted to complain and beg to go home, but every time she took a big enough breath to start, enough pain ripped through her chest to quiet her once more.

Kyla huffed. Josh had just stepped out for a vending machine run, and if the last four hours of awkward rotation taught her anything, Dylan was incoming. Three... Two...

Dylan poked his head in the door. She nodded. He sidled in and took the chair Josh had just vacated. A rerun of some sitcom she'd heard of but never seen before blared on the TV. Nobody had seen fit to give her a remote. As with every other rotation, Dylan didn't say anything, and Kyla had reached her breaking point.

"So, what? Are we just not friends anymore? Why are you here then?" she demanded.

He turned to her slowly. "Well, I did think certain yellings and leavings implied we were in a bad spot."

"If we're in a bad spot, you can't just come and sit in my hospital room." Tears welled in Kyla's eyes. She hadn't forgiven Dylan, but she couldn't exactly bring herself to want him to go.

"I don't—" Dylan closed his eyes and inhaled slowly, then after blowing out a deep breath, he opened his eyes and looked at her. "I don't want to give up on us, but I didn't think you were in any kind of shape to be hashing out the mess I got us in."

Kyla inhaled, then winced. She wasn't in any kind of shape to do anything, but she also didn't know how to go home with all her relationships up in the air.

"Did you hear anything about the...accident?" she asked.

Dylan cleared his throat. "The fire's out. Search and Rescue found a body."

Her ribs ached. Or maybe that was her heart.

"I don't exactly have jurisdiction, but the size seemed right," he said.

On instinct, Kyla reached for his hand. Dylan moved to take it, then recoiled slightly.

"Rosy, I don't think—"

"Yeah." She suddenly felt exhausted again.

A tinny laugh track sounded on the TV, and Dylan averted his attention. Kyla pulled the scratchy hospital blanket up to her chin and tried not to feel like her best friend had just broken up with her.

"I'm sorry." Dylan didn't take his gaze off the TV. "For all of it. Alan. The part I played. The stuff with Josh."

"But we can't just go back, can we?" Kyla's voice broke on the last word, and she watched the corner of Dylan's mouth twitch upward.

"Not yet," he said.

"I miss you." The moment she said the words, she wished she could take them back. Dylan's face contorted into a grimace, and if she didn't know any better, she'd say tears threatened in the corners of his eyes.

"I miss you too, Rosy. More than I can say. But I think my brother could make you really happy." Without turning, Dylan took her hand and pressed a soft kiss to its back, then put it down. "You deserve to be happy."

Kyla barely caught a sob in her throat. "I don't want to be happy without you."

Dylan smiled ruefully. "I should've known you'd make the noble path difficult."

"Are you mad at him?" Her voice was an embarrassing squeak.

"How could I blame him for falling for the perfect woman?" Dylan scrubbed a hand across his face. "I don't want to be mad at him. I'm going to try not to be, for a change. But, Rosy, I'm gonna need time."

She nodded. She didn't want to cry, didn't want to guilt him into staying. Well, she did a little, but she'd never forgive herself if that was what she ended up doing.

"Dill?"

"Yeah?"

"I'll be here whenever you're ready."

Josh rapped on the glass of her window, and Dylan shot out of his seat. Her heart thudded as they exchanged places silently. Kyla didn't want to be the reason why Josh didn't have a brother.

As Dylan stepped out and a nurse stepped in, he looked back at them and smiled.

She needed that smile in her life. She needed her best friend. However, she wasn't sure she could call herself Dylan's best friend if she chose to date Josh, ruining the brothers' relationship forever.

Kyla had a lot of thinking to do.

CHAPTER THIRTY-THREE

By the time Kyla got released from the hospital, Josh had started to regret his insistence on being the one to drive her home. He hadn't slept more than five minutes in the last two days, and he felt like somebody had rubbed sand into his eyes. That, coupled with Kyla's continuing refusal to give him a straight answer, did not make for a pleasant four-hour drive.

"Are you all right?" Kyla asked. She sat stiffly in the passenger's seat, hopefully just because her ribs were sore and not because she'd have any long-term fear of cars.

Josh tried to grin, but the expression felt tight on his face. "Shouldn't I be asking you that?"

She sighed heavily. "It's been a long week."

Thor whuffed in agreement. Tiff and Jer had shown up at the hospital as Kyla was being discharged and had traded the dog for giving Dylan a ride back to the car he'd abandoned. Dylan had asked Kyla to take the dog home, which only made Josh more confused. He wanted to demand straight answers, but it was hard to hold on to his frustration when Kyla winced at every bump in the road.

"My feelings don't seem like a big deal right now. You went

through something traumatic, and I wish I could hold you and make it better." Josh tightened his hands around the steering wheel. Stupid, stupid. "If you wanted me to."

Out of the corner of his eye, he watched Kyla swipe away a fresh wave of tears. Maybe one day he'd stop making this woman cry.

"I'm sorry," she mumbled.

"No, no. Please don't be sorry. I know this is complicated, and I don't want to pressure you." Didn't he use to be smooth? Hadn't he won scores of women over with his words? He felt like such an idiot.

"I just"—Kyla sniffled—"think we need some time to sort this out."

He nodded as if her words hadn't felt like another punch to the head. Time. Time would only give her the chance to realize he really had been a waste of her energy and find someone easier to date. She'd get to keep Dylan, and Josh would get to nurse a hangover for the next six months.

The rest of the drive passed in silence, except when Thor got excited about the scenery. Finally, they pulled up outside her apartment as a golden sunset poked rays through heavy cloud cover.

"Let me carry your bags," he said. Maybe it'd be more than six months.

"I only have my camera. Everything else is in the ditch." She grimaced at the thought.

"I've got it anyway." Even knowing she probably wouldn't give him the time of day in any given week, he couldn't help but try to spend as much time with her as possible. How had he fallen in love so quickly?

Kyla leashed the dog, offered Josh a small smile of thanks, and slowly led the way up three flights of stairs.

"You're spending the night with me," she said as Thor angled for Dylan's door.

"Lucky guy," Josh muttered. Being jealous of a dog was definitely beneath him, but that didn't stop the feeling from pooling in his stomach.

Kyla stopped at the door across the hall. "This is me."

Josh handed her the backpack and willed himself to leave. Instead, he found his mouth moving. "Are you sure you should be alone right now?"

Kyla sighed again. "I don't know, Josh. But I know I need some space to think."

He leaned against the wall, trying to look casual. "I could just sit on the sofa, stay out of your way?"

She smiled softly and wrapped her arms around his waist. His heart broke. There was no misunderstanding what Kyla was going to do now. She was saying goodbye.

He hugged her back delicately, trying not to hurt her any worse, then pressed a kiss to the top of her head.

Of course, she pulled back first. He shoved his hands in his pockets for something to do.

"You have my number if you change your mind." His voice sounded gruff.

She nodded. "Thank you."

There was nothing for him here. Not his brother, and not the woman he'd fallen in love with. He turned on his heel. "See you around."

Kyla's door opened and closed behind her.

* * *

A WEEK AND A HALF HAD PASSED—MORE TIME THAN HE'D SPENT WITH Kyla in the first place. He hadn't heard a peep from her or Dylan, and at this point, he didn't expect to. He woke feeling like he'd been run over by a truck and rolled out of bed to begin his day.

His early morning staff was already at the bakery when Josh arrived. The past week had been the first time in his life that he hadn't cared about the bakery, but he tried to show up at least.

His kitchen manager, Romeo, had begun filling the display case with the rocky road cookies Josh had concocted before the trip. "Hey, boss. How's the morning treating you?"

Josh laughed bitterly and shook his head. "Better than I deserve." He looked at the cooling rack full of freshly baked peanut butter cookies. "Smells good in here."

Romeo looked him over. "No offense, boss, but you look awful."

"I haven't slept." He'd barely gotten an hour's rest since leaving Kyla, as if that one endless night had ruined him forever.

"Girl trouble?" Romeo asked.

"You could say that again."

"Hope it clears up soon. Next up are the chocolate chips." With that, Romeo turned away to line baking sheets. Josh sighed, washed up, and began the chocolate chip batter.

The day passed in a blur. He gave himself the small luxury of only making the easiest recipes so his mind could wander.

He couldn't picture Kyla without seeing the hurt on her face when she left the cabin, and the quick swipe of tears on the ride home from the hospital.

A small part of him still hoped she'd cared, even a little. That she thought about the fun they had shared up at the cabin before Alan ruined everything. Josh also hoped she missed him and sometimes regretted choosing Dylan. She shouldn't have to choose, though. It wasn't fair for her. She should be able to follow her heart and not have to pick one brother over the other.

Maybe he only thought that way because she hadn't chosen him.

Sometime after lunch, Josh found himself robotically working the register when a small army of kids with moms in tow exploded into his bakery. He sighed. He should have expected this when he set up so close to a park, but this was the first summer the families that frequented the park had really noticed the shop. He handled the rush with practiced ease but a great deal less than his usual charm and tried to block out the hollering.

However, when the hollering turned to proper screaming, he couldn't help but notice. A little girl, maybe six, had been playing tag with her brother when she'd run headfirst into a high-topped metal table Josh kept at the front of the shop for those who wanted to enjoy their pastries on the spot. A nasty bruise began to form on her forehead, and she screamed as if she were dying.

With instincts he didn't know he had, Josh sprang into action. He made his apologies to the dad at the counter, then bundled a few cubes of ice into a spare towel. Romeo had used up the last of the bandages yesterday, and Josh had only been able to find kiddie ones at the drugstore this morning, so he scooped up the box and scooted to where the little girl sat. Her mother squatted nearby, clearly on the phone with someone she'd left at the park with their bag. Josh gestured with his hodgepodge of medical offerings, and she nodded. He turned to the little girl.

Her face had nearly turned red with the exertion of her screaming, but she watched him with careful eyes as he sat.

"Hi," he said. "My name's Josh, and I make all the cookies here. I see you got hurt. Can I help?"

The girl sniffled, then rubbed one of her eyes. "Can I have a cookie if I let you?"

Josh chuckled. "Of course. Whichever is your favorite. Now, I've got some ice here. If you put that on your forehead, it should hurt less. Can I?"

The girl wrinkled her nose suspiciously but nodded. "My favorite's all of 'em. Can I have all of 'em?"

"You drive a hard bargain, but I think your mom wouldn't like that very much. How about we pick you out two for being so brave?"

The little girl smiled a gapped-toothed smile at him, and Josh felt happy for the first time since he'd left Kyla's door. He'd never really understood the appeal of kids before, but he thought he got it now.

After getting the girl her cookies and a dino bandage, he finished off the rush in a much better mood. He was even whistling when a petite brunette with her hair piled on top of her head strode up to him. Most customers lingered, perusing the bakery case before finally deciding, but this woman didn't even hesitate.

"Josh? Hamilton?" she asked.

Josh blinked twice. "Yeah?

She grinned at him and handed over a folded piece of notebook paper. Then, she turned on her heel and left.

Josh shook his head. What just happened? He unfolded the paper to see a short, handwritten message.

Ten Spoon Vineyard. Midnight.

He looked up in time to see the woman walk past his plate glass windows. A camera bag bounced against her hip.

Realization dawned, and Josh grinned.

CHAPTER THIRTY-FOUR

KYLA LEANED HEAVILY AGAINST A WEDDING ARCH ENCRUSTED WITH flowers. Before her, she could just make out the grounds of Ten Spoon Vineyard. The place had been beautiful when Phil and Kiera exchanged their vows that afternoon, but now, lit with nothing more than the fading twinkles of a few fairy lights, it felt enchanted.

She inhaled and exhaled slowly, trying to keep her head. She had nothing to worry about. A quick check of her phone told her it was only eleven-fifty. He'd show.

Andrea traipsed up the small hill to the arch where Kyla waited, grinning wildly. "Phil and Kiera just loaded into the limo. I got some great shots. They did bubbles instead of rice. Very cute." She glanced around. "No sign yet?"

Kyla shook her head. She'd finally gotten to a friendly enough place with Dylan that they could trade Thor back and forth without wincing. They would be friends again someday, she felt certain. She'd taken some time to herself to grieve Alan, or at least start to. She had good memories of him, good times, but it would take work to rectify that with how things ended.

Now, she finally felt ready to move on. To pick up where she and Josh had left off.

If he would have her.

The note had been Andrea's idea, of course. Kyla had wanted to go to his place and talk to him, but this cloak-and-dagger thing was "far more romantic."

Kyla mostly deemed it was far more stress-inducing.

Andrea shrugged. "He'll be here. When I saw him, he looked like a total zombie, and there's only one thing that messes a guy up like that. Love."

Kyla snorted, which sent another spike of pain through her chest. She winced and put a hand to her ribs. "This would be much more romantic if I could reliably stand upright."

"You win some. You lose some." Andrea stepped closer and began fussing with Kyla's hair. "You sure you want me to scram when he gets here? I could get some really gorgeous shots of you in this lighting."

Kyla resisted the urge to elbow her. "Positive."

Somebody cleared their throat behind Andrea. She spun away to reveal Josh with hands shoved deep in his pockets. Kyla's heart started beating double-time, and she blushed.

"Hi," she said.

"Hey," Josh answered.

Andrea squealed, and Kyla waved her away. She pouted but scurried back the way she came.

Josh looked beautiful under these lights, as she'd known he would. His eyes glistened like sapphires, and she wanted nothing more than to kiss him. She stepped forward. He was within arm's reach.

"What's all this?" He stared around at the tableau she'd created.

"There was a wedding here this afternoon. I didn't want the decorations to go to waste."

A smile tugged at the corner of his lips, but he flattened his mouth into a line. Right. She couldn't just kiss him and make everything better.

"I asked you to come here because I wanted to tell you something."

Josh quirked an eyebrow.

"I wanted to tell you I'm scared. I'm scared of this, us. How I feel about you." Kyla steadied herself on the arch again. Josh stared down at her, and she wanted to skip this part and just get lost in his eyes. "But I think I've been scared for a long time before this. I told you my mom stayed with my dad after he cheated, but I never told you why. I asked her once, just after I graduated college. She got misty-eyed and told me he was the love of her life. She'd never find someone better. I was scared of falling in love like that. Of setting myself up to get hurt forever like her. But I come here, I do my job, and it's hard not to fall in love with the idea of love. The look of it." She took his hand. "I've been chasing things that look like love my whole life. Alan looked a lot like love."

Josh snorted, and she squeezed his hand. If she didn't get through this now, she never would. He stayed silent.

"Then you appeared in an empty cabin, and you looked like fun." Josh blanched, but she plowed forward. "I didn't know I was supposed to protect myself from fun. Hell, I barely knew I was supposed to have it. But Josh, you're so much more than that. I... I've fallen in real, scary love with you."

Josh's head tipped back, and he laughed. For a moment, rejection tore through her body. Then, he closed the distance between them and kissed her the way he had in the rain, and she also wanted to laugh.

When he pulled back, he whispered, "I've fallen for you, too."

A welcome giggle burst from her lips. She would have spun in a circle if it hadn't meant letting go of him for too long.

"Already?" She ran her hands over his cheeks before burying her fingers into his hair. Josh didn't even try to hold back his groan of pleasure and relief at her touch.

He kissed her again. "Yes, already. You are extremely easy to fall for." Another kiss. "But I could ask you the same thing. Already?"

She pressed her lips hard against his. "Already."

Kyla could have stood under the lights with Josh forever, but too soon, he pulled back with worry in his eyes.

"What about Dylan?"

"We talked." She rested her head against his chest, not wanting to be any farther away. "He just needs time."

Josh pressed a kiss to the top of her head, and she leaned back to look at him. Someday, she'd be able to have everything she wanted, but for now, she needed to know if she had him.

"So, Josh Hamilton, do you want to give this dating thing a try?"

He beamed at her, that crooked grin she'd grown to love. "I really, really do."

She slid her hands under his T-shirt. "I just hope relationship sex is as great as rebound sex."

EPILOGUE

"You're finally here!" Kyla could have danced up the stairs to her—their apartment if she hadn't laden herself with duffel bags of Josh's clothes. His lease had run out at the end of the month, and unlike Alan, he'd jumped at the chance to move in when she asked.

Even carrying bags up the stairs, having him here felt like a weight off her shoulders. Scheduling had been a nightmare over the last three months between their busy work schedules, but if she could wake up next to Josh every morning? She'd have all the time in the world to stare at those broad shoulders, that sharp jawline, and those laughing eyes. She could bask in his mere presence over breakfast.

Kyla had been worried about fitting all of Josh's things in, but since Dylan had sold her wedding dress before his disastrous appearance at the cabin, Josh had plenty of room.

She didn't need the past anymore. She had an amazing future ahead of her.

Josh followed her off the stairs and set down a huge box of cookware outside the door, then fished his shiny new key from his front pocket and held it up with a grin.

"This is it." He slid the key into the lock and turned.

"Welcome home," she said as he stepped inside the apartment and dropped another of his duffle bags on the floor.

He pulled her into his arms, pressed their bodies together, and leaned down to kiss her lips. "Home sweet home is right."

She laughed. "How much is left in the Jeep?"

"Lots." He shrugged. "Dylan said he would be here."

Kyla stood on tiptoes to kiss away the frown lines that settled between his eyebrows. "He will be."

Josh huffed. "Your endless optimism is a turn-on."

She smiled and rubbed his back. "Don't change the subject. We'll christen the place once you've settled in."

He hummed and buried his face in the crook of her neck, breathed in her skin. "You're all the home I need."

"You're still the best flirt I know." She pressed a kiss to his temple.

"It's so easy around you, sexy lady."

A throat cleared in the hallway behind them, and they both turned to look at Dylan, pizza in his hand, a case of beer under his arm, and Thor sitting at his side. "If this whole day is going to be a live porno, I'm going to turn around and eat this pizza with my dog across the hall."

"Why didn't you warn me about the neighbors?" Josh asked.

"Ha, ha." Dylan squeezed her arm, then punched Josh's shoulder. "Welcome to the building, baby bro."

"Thanks."

"Had to work late." Dylan moved past them and into the kitchen. Thor flopped down on the couch.

Josh winked at her and followed his brother. He took the case, pulled out a few bottles, and slotted it into an empty spot in the fridge.

Kyla hovered near the door. The brothers exchanged a few

tense sentences, then Dylan broke out in laughter, and Josh joined him. Awkward laughter, but laughter all the same.

She grinned.

Over the last few months, Josh had mentioned Dylan occasionally, but she could tell he missed his brother more than he let on. She figured he didn't want her to feel guilty for her part in the most recent rift in their relationship. It had been her idea for Josh to ask Dylan to help them move. As Josh told the story, there had been a long pause on the line before Dylan agreed, but he'd shown.

As Dylan clapped his brother on the shoulder, she realized she no longer felt guilty. They'd all been hurt, but now she and Josh had a beautiful future ahead of them with Dylan in it.

Josh sauntered over and caressed her fingers. "We're going down for another load."

"Sounds good," she said. "I'll guard the pizza."

Josh left, and Dylan came up behind her. She turned.

"You happy?" he asked.

She looked up at her best friend and smiled. "I am," she said truthfully. "I'm even happier you're here."

"Yeah?" His eyebrows twitched in disbelief. "Even after everything?"

She closed her eyes. Kyla missed spending evenings on Dylan's couch, and she definitely regretted some of the things she said up at the cabin, but she couldn't find it in herself to be upset anymore.

She looked back up at him, then wrapped her arms around his waist. He hesitated for a moment, then returned the hug. She hadn't felt his arms around her since the night of the accident.

"I love you, Dylan. I always will."

"Don't get mushy on me," he said. She studied his face. His

eyes had filled with unshed tears. "I love you, too, Kyla. You know that, right?"

She nodded, tearing up herself. "It wouldn't have felt right without you here. To either of us."

He smiled ruefully. "To me either."

Loud footsteps sounded on the stairs, and Josh said, "I thought I was getting help?"

"Right." Dylan brushed the back of his hand over his eyes, then walked out the door.

"You okay?" Josh managed to look concerned while balancing a state-of-the-art blender in one hand and yet another duffel bag in the other.

Kyla grinned tearfully. "I couldn't be better."

Josh smiled and set his things down inside. "Andrea's downstairs."

"Ah. Part two of my epic plan is unfolding."

Josh pressed a kiss to her lips. "You have the biggest heart of anyone I know."

"Have you not met Thor?" she asked, glancing over at the now seventy-pound dog asleep upside down on her sofa.

"When should we tell Dylan about the engagement?"

The news had been bubbling behind her lips all morning, but today was a big step for Dylan. For all of them. She didn't want to ruin it in her excitement. "Soon," she said. "He'll be happy for us."

"You sure?"

She nodded. "I know it."

Josh gathered her in his arms and pressed a hot kiss to her lips. The urgency of his mouth, the hum of desire, made her wish for time to fly. Their first night together awaited.

Josh spun them around the room, dancing between boxes.

"What are you doing?" she asked.

"It's just an excuse to hold my fiancée."

She'd get used to that eventually, but right now, her heart raced. Last night, she'd been his girlfriend, alone with him in his bakery as they tested the new heart-shaped cookies. This morning, she moved him in as his fiancée.

Kyla added an extra twirl to Josh's dance.

"Since when did you need an excuse to hold me?"

"Maybe I just like watching you move. I haven't seen you dance since the week I met you."

She snorted a laugh. "I did no such thing."

Josh laughed and kissed her. "You twirled in the rain. That counts."

"After I let you get to third base in the Jeep when I was outside without a bra? Your memory is clouded."

"I'll never forget that week, Kyla," he said. "It changed my life."

She smiled. She couldn't do anything else in his arms. "For the better?"

Josh dipped her low and stole a kiss. "For the very best."

SNEAK PEEK AT READY TO BURN BY MANDY MICHELLE

CHAPTER ONE

Ronan stirred his latest creation over the kitchen stove in Firehouse 3 and called, "Who wants chili?"

Lieutenant Keith Murphy stepped up, bowl in hand. "Always, McGuire."

Ronan poured a ladleful into his superior's dish and laughed when Keith nodded for a second helping.

The lieutenant tasted the chili then raised his brows. "This is the shit. Is this what you're going with for this year's chili cookoff?"

"Something like it," Ronan said. "I'm determined to beat the guys from Firehouse 4 this year."

"Well, whatever you're doing, keep it up, man."

Ronan grinned. "Glad to hear my cooking classes haven't been a waste of time." Attending culinary school between shifts had been a helluva challenge and didn't leave time for much of a social life, but he enjoyed it.

"Well, whatever you're doing, keep it up." The lieutenant stuffed a heaping spoonful into his mouth. "You excited for tonight, McGuire?"

Five more guys on shift filed in and Ronan filled another

bowl, tossed grated cheddar on top, and slid it down the counter to Mike Sheppard. "No, sir."

"Is our virgin nervous for his first time?" Mike grabbed the ladle from Ronan, heaped more chili atop the cheese, then dug in.

"You were the virgin last year, Sheppard." Diego Fuentes slapped Mike's back. "And if I remember correctly, pretty damn thin."

Ronan filled Diego's bowl. "Just how thin was he?"

Ronan filled three more bowls before getting his own, then joined the men at the table. He scooped up a spoonful of chili.

The fire alarm blared.

Ronan groaned. Happened every time.

Mike wolfed down another bite, then dropped the spoon with a clatter as Ronan twisted off the knobs on the stove. Both men turned in unison, hurried through the door, and took a quick left into the truck bay.

Ronan stepped into his turnout pants, slung on his jacket, and grabbed his helmet. He jumped through the truck's open side door as the lieutenant turned over the engine and flipped on the sirens.

Ronan, shoulder to shoulder with Rogers, bowed his head in a quick prayer. He took a deep breath to calm his pounding heart. Each call always felt like the first.

They pulled away from the firehouse. In less than three minutes, Ronan caught sight of black smoke rising into the sky from somewhere in a residential neighborhood to the west. The fire truck turned onto Westminster Road. The smoke seemed to come from one of the older homes behind Henderson Point.

Keith halted the truck in front of a two-story house where bright red flames lapped at the fresh winter air through the broken windows of a detached garage. Thick clouds of black smoke spiralled heavenward. The garage siding had begun to melt and blacken. The flames hadn't spread to the house. Yet. The house sat only twenty feet from the garage and could catch in a matter of minutes.

Half the neighborhood stood across the street with phones outstretched to record the action.

"We're going to be online, again," Diego muttered. "Look sharp out there, guys."

"Diego and Sheppard on hose," the lieutenant ordered. "Peters, clear the house. McGuire and I will secure the perimeter."

The men sprang into action.

"Fire Department." Ronan jogged across the street toward the onlookers. "Anyone inside?"

"Manny's away on a big demolition job," someone said.

"Away?" Ronan blurted.

A man nodded. "Manny owns J & M Demolition and they have a big job down south. He lives alone, so no one's in the house."

Ronan whirled and called "Thanks!" over his shoulder as he hurried back across the street toward the fire truck.

Water arced from the hose of the deck gun that Mike and Diego directed at the garage. Billows of white steam poured from the garage as water hit the flames. Ronan teamed with the lieutenant to pull a hose from the truck. In seconds, they had a stream of water directed at the doorway. With a bang, the door blew back on its hinges and slammed against the wall of the garage. Onlookers screamed.

The heat, God, that heat seeped through Ronan's protective gear and into his body. Sweat rolled down his back as he widened his stance to brace against the pressure of the water and directed the heavy stream to douse the flames. Others on the team used hand lines to wet down the home, fences, and the neighbor's garage to keep the fire from spreading.

Hours later, they had the fire controlled. Diego strode to the right side of the garage with a halogen—a crowbar on steroids —and fitted the end into a crack in the wall and pulled back the siding. Oxygen-fueled embers burst into flames. Diego threw up an arm to protect his face and stumbled back several paces as Ronan sprayed water into the new access point.

Another long hour later, they had the fire extinguished and the lieutenant cut the water to Ronan's hose. The ache in his arms had gone numb from overuse. Ronan rolled his shoulders. An hour from now, the ache would return with a vengeance.

While the rest of the crew stowed gear, Ronan headed back to the garage. Today was December 31, two weeks to the day since the fire on Lenore Street, another house where the owner had been away when their home caught fire. This was the fourth fire in six weeks, each exactly two weeks apart, where the owners had been away. Well, the owner of the house on Hedge Lane had been home, but he'd returned a day earlier than expected and was asleep when his home's fire alarm went off. He'd gotten his wife and daughter out but had sustained burns to his arms and face.

The fire marshal would assess the damage and cause of the fire, but Ronan wanted to know if this fire was connected to the other three fires. The first had been a faulty gas line, the second, electrical, and the third, a can of lighter fluid that the fire marshal ruled that someone had slung through a garage window.

Separately, there was nothing connecting the fires. But the fact that the owners weren't home—or weren't supposed to be home—bugged Ronan. Not to mention, each fire had occurred exactly two weeks apart.

Ronan reached the garage and carefully stepped over debris that had fallen at the entrance. Blackened rubble of the half-walled, roofless structure crunched under his steel toe boots.

Everything inside the garage had burned. Ronan identified the remains of a melted plastic gas can on the property. As he started to turn away, he spotted what looked like a shattered beer bottle near the rear of the garage. He exited through the front door and strode around the garage to the glass. Ronan toed through the debris and found what he was looking for: the bottle cap. He rubbed the ash off the surface with his thumb and recognized the brand: Red Cap.

Keith joined him. "Not good, huh?"

Ronan rubbed his stiff neck. "No."

"The fire investigator is on her way." Keith shrugged. "Our work's done. Plus, you don't want to catch more flack for mucking up a fire scene."

Ronan grimaced. He wouldn't soon forget that stripping down from Fire Marshal Kate O'Malley last month. She might be a five-foot-nothing blonde, but she was no pushover. She'd probably love nothing more than to see him fired. She liked order, and he had a way of messing that up for her.

Ronan stared at the house. "Two weeks on the dot."

"Don't start," the lieutenant said.

"The fires are connected, Lieutenant. I feel it in my gut."

"We don't solve crimes, McGuire. We put out fires. You have a bigger problem, anyway."

Ronan frowned. "What's that?"

"A room full of rowdy women."

Ronan groaned and rubbed his face. Call him crazy, but he would rather investigate this fire than face a bar full of horny firemen groupies. Even if that investigation meant dealing with O'Malley.

A pair of hands landed hard on his shoulders and he smiled before he turned around. "Hey, Janis." Thank God those hands belonged to his favorite policewoman and not the fire marshal. This woman liked him.

"You went in, didn't you?" Her casual voice didn't fool him for a minute. "I told you to stick to your job and just put out the fires."

"That's exactly what I did, officer." He winked and flashed his most charming smile.

Her eyes narrowed. "You know what I mean."

He had known Detective Janis Rylands of the Rapid Falls Police Department since high school. They had dated during their sophomore year, back when she was Janis Simmons. She had married an accountant, of all people, and was happier than he had ever seen her. A hell of a lot more confident, too.

"This has me worried, Janis." He stared at her face and frowned. "You look a little green. You feeling okay?"

She grimaced. "Let's just say, morning sickness isn't just for mornings."

"You're pregnant?" Ronan grinned. "Congratulations. You're going to be a stellar mom."

She laughed then grimaced again. "Thanks. Don't spread the word around the firehall, okay? It's early."

"Done deal," Ronan said. "Be careful out here, huh?"

"I'm always careful, McGuire. And nice subject change."

He drew an x over his heart. "I promise not to set foot in another crime scene."

She laughed, which made her appear sixteen again. "You're such a bad liar. Oh, and have fun tonight with the ladies."

"I will."

She shook her head. "A damn bad liar."

CHAPTER TWO

Alison approached Andie's Pub and, even through the closed door, heard laughter and music. Another busy New Year's Eve. She entered and hurried to the bar where the owner, Joey, poured drinks and her boss, Megan, hoisted a full tray of cocktails over her shoulder.

"Thanks for coming in, Ali. We're swamped." Megan turned on her kitten heels and shook her shapely hips as she walked to a table of noisy women.

As the co-owner, Megan normally ran the numbers in her office, kept the stock room full, and juggled the schedule. But tonight called for all hands on deck.

Alison hurried to the office and put her purse and keys in the lower desk drawer before heading back to the bar. In her five years on staff, Alison had never seen Andie's so full. It was close to bursting at the seams—and with good reason.

Tonight was the big reveal of the Rapid Falls Firefighters Charity Calendar. Megan was lucky to have landed the exclusive event at her bar. The proceeds from calendar sales went to charity, but the drink sales were all Andie's. The best part, the tips belonged to the servers. Monday was Alison's usual night off, but with Roseanne out sick, Alison was quick to fill in. Huge profits could be made off the single and not-so-single ladies trying to catch the attention of sexy firemen. Throw a half-naked man in the room and, *voila*, the purse strings were loosened.

All the small pubs in town had rallied for the right to host the twelve sexy calendar boys. Meg's place had won out. The stage had been a major selling point, but the seating capacity had sealed the deal.

Besides the logistics, Megan deserved the honor. Not only had she built this place from the ground up while her husband served overseas, she'd managed to keep the doors open during Joey's six-month recovery at the veterans' hospital in the next town over. She was strong, brave, and one heck of a boss. A boss who had become Alison's best friend and biggest supporter.

Tonight, the firemen were volunteering their time, too. They were sweet to do this for charity. Heck, they probably didn't mind having their egos stroked, either. Most were probably hoping to go home with a big breasted consolation prize, so Alison doubted any of them would complain.

An eighty-something-year-old woman sitting at the nearest table to the left signaled her. Alison hurried to her table. "Hey, honey, I'll take another *Quick Fuck*."

Alison winced inwardly at the colorful cocktail name which was Megan's pride and joy. She and Joey had searched to the ends of the earth to find the most vulgar cocktail names for tonight's event. The couple were nothing if not dedicated.

"I'll be right back with that." Alison smiled, then headed back to the bar through the mass of bodies and howling laughter. She didn't even have her apron on yet. God, these women were wild with the promise of testosterone and a little chest hair.

"You look nauseous already, Ali." Joey winked a dark, chocolate-brown eye.

Meg's husband was such a damn comedian, and she loved him for it. She needed to laugh off her discomfort.

He twirled a bottle of vodka in that artful way only bartenders trained in the nineteen eighties could pull off. "What do you need, little lady?"

"I don't know why your cocktails have such ridiculous names." She rolled her eyes to distract attention from her blush.

"It is all because of you horny women, Ms. Walker. You keep us bartenders in business."

"A *Quick Fuck*," she said.

Joey laughed, and his eyes shone with mischief. "What was that, Ali? I couldn't hear you. It's so damn loud in here."

Alison reached over the marble bar for her black apron and tied it around her waist, all while skillfully avoiding Joey's eyes. "You heard me."

"Alison." Joey poured himself a shot of vodka. He slung it back, gave a satisfying "ahh," and slammed the glass down. "This stuff ain't cheap. I don't want to make the wrong drink." Another of his teasing winks accompanied his lecture.

God, she hated this man for making her say it out loud.

"Joey. I need a *Quick Fuck*."

Amidst Joey's laughter, a deep male voice behind her said, "Maybe I can help with that."

A warm hand pressed her lower back. Alison started at the heat that flashed through her. Oh, no. She couldn't let herself bask in the male attention sure to overflow tonight. She couldn't afford to. Not anymore.

"You wish," she shot back without looking at him.

He gave a low laugh, as if he did wish for it.

The heat headed south. Great. His warm, rich voice would

surely melt her butter. She wouldn't even get started on his delicious, husky laughter.

Alison whirled to tell the man to get lost, but her mouth went dry as her eyeline slammed into a tight, navy t-shirt stretched over muscled pecs. The Rapid Falls Fire Department logo left no mistake about who had propositioned her. One of the guests of honor. One of the men who had donated his New Year's Eve for the county's sick children.

She was a mother. He was a hero.

Alison bit her tongue. She couldn't be rude to a man who saved lives. Instead, she embarrassed herself by keeping her gaze on his chest and stammering, "It's...it's a cocktail."

Her pulse kicked up. What kind of cocktail waitress couldn't handle the word cocktail?

Alison faced the bar and said, "All right then. That's one *Quick Fuck* for me and one for the firefighter, please, Joey."

Without looking at his face, Alison turned on her tip-earning heels, a trick honed from years of practice, and headed for the table. She had a sweet baby girl at home who counted on these paychecks to keep her in diapers, cute onesies, and of course, adorable shoes. Like mother, like daughter.

The novelty clock on the wall told her she had four hours left until midnight. Four hours left to avoid flirtatious firefighters who made her question her decision to avoid men. She would have to look at the situation glass half full. Half full of a *Quick Fuck*.

www.ingramcontent.com/pod-product-compliance
Lightning Source LLC
Chambersburg PA
CBHW060713190726
48289CB00002B/658